BERNARD MALAMUD

GOD'S GRACE

"*GOD'S GRACE* IS A STORY
BLESSED WITH DRAMA, HUMOR AND PATHOS...
MALAMUD IS A SUPERB STORYTELLER...FROM
THE SIMPLEST AND CLEAREST OF STYLES
HE PRODUCES THE MOST INTENSE EMOTIONS."

NEWSDAY

"TOUCHING AND BEAUTIFUL...
MALAMUD'S PASSIONS AND COMMITMENTS
ARE SO DECENT AND ELOQUENT."

PHILADELPHIA INQUIRER

Other Avon Books by
Bernard Malamud

THE ASSISTANT
DUBIN'S LIVES
THE MAGIC BARREL
THE NATURAL
A NEW LIFE
THE TENANTS

GOD'S GRACE

BERNARD MALAMUD

AVON
PUBLISHERS OF BARD, CAMELOT, DISCUS AND FLARE BOOKS

AVON BOOKS
A division of
The Hearst Corporation
959 Eighth Avenue
New York, New York 10019

Published by arrangement with Farrar, Straus & Giroux, Inc.
Library of Congress Catalog Card Number: 82-11880
ISBN: 0-380-64519-x

The Farrar, Straus & Giroux, Inc. edition contains the following Library of Congress Cataloging in Publication Data:

Malamud, Bernard.
God's grace.
I. Title.
PS3563.A4G6 1982 813′.54 82-11880

First Avon Printing, October, 1983

Printed in the U. S. A.

WFH 10 9 8 7 6 5 4 3 2 1

FOR DIARMUID RUSSELL

GONE NOW;

AND FOR ROSE RUSSELL

I'm grateful to the Center for Advanced Study in the Behavioral Sciences for gifts of time and hospitality; and to Carol Bain, Del Powers, and Deanna Dejan for secretarial and word-processing assistance; and to Eleanor Moore, who typed early drafts of this story in Bennington, Vermont.

I read many books to write this but am particularly indebted to Shalom Spiegel's *The Last Trial*, and Jane Goodall's *In the Shadow of Man*.

The Holy One, blessed be He, cast a stone into the sea and from it the world was founded.

R. YITZHAQ NAPPAHA

I came upon the horrible remains of a cannibal feast.

ROBINSON CRUSOE

Nobody seemed to know where George's name came from.

JOHANSON, EDEY

The Flood

This is that story

The heaving high seas were laden with scum

The dull sky glowed red

Dust and ashes drifted in the wind circling the earth

The burdened seas slanted this way, and that, flooding the scorched land under a daylight moon

A black oily rain rained

No one was there

At the end, after the thermonuclear war between the Djanks and Druzhkies, in consequence of which they had destroyed themselves, and, madly, all other inhabitants of the earth, God spoke through a glowing crack in a bulbous black cloud to Calvin Cohn, the paleologist, who of all men had miraculously survived in a battered oceanography vessel with sails, as the swollen seas tilted this way and that;

Saying this:

""Don't presume on Me a visible face, Mr. Cohn, I am not that kind, but if you can, imagine Me. I regret to say it was through a minuscule error that you escaped destruction. Though mine, it was not a serious one; a serious mistake might have jammed the universe. The cosmos is so conceived that I myself don't know what goes on everywhere. It is not perfection although I, of course, am perfect. That's how I arranged my mind.

""And that you, Mr. Cohn, happen to exist when no one else does, though embarrassing to Me, has nothing to do with your once having studied for the rabbinate, or for that matter, having given it up.

""That was your concern, but I don't want you to conceive any false expectations. Inevitably, my purpose is to rectify the error I conceived.

""I have no wish to torment you, only once more affirm cause and effect. It is no more than a system within a system, yet I depend on it to maintain a certain order. Man, after failing to use to a sufficient purpose his possibilities, and my good will, has destroyed himself; therefore, in truth, so have you.""

Cohn, shivering in his dripping rubber diving suit, complained bitterly:

"After Your first Holocaust You promised no further Floods. ""Never again shall there be a Flood to destroy the earth."" That was Your Covenant with Noah and all living creatures. Instead, You turned the water on again. Everyone who wasn't consumed in fire is drowned in bitter water, and a Second Flood covers the earth."

God said this: ""All that was pre-Torah. There was no such thing as Holocaust, only cause and effect. But after I had created man I did not know how he would fail Me next, in what matter of violence, corruption, blasphemy, beastliness, sin beyond belief. Thus he defiled himself. I had not foreseen the extent of it.

""The present Devastation, ending in smoke and dust, comes as a consequence of man's self-betrayal. From the beginning, when I gave them the gift of life, they were perversely greedy for death. At last I thought, I will give them death because they are engrossed in evil.

""They have destroyed my handiwork, the conditions of their survival: the sweet air I gave them to breathe; the fresh water I blessed them with, to drink and bathe in; the fertile green earth. They tore apart my ozone, carbonized my oxygen, acidified my refreshing rain. Now they affront my cosmos. How much shall the Lord endure?

""I made man to be free, but his freedom, badly used, destroyed him. In sum, the evil overwhelmed the good. The Second Flood, this that now subsides on the broken earth, they brought on themselves. They had not lived according to the Covenant.

""Therefore I let them do away with themselves. They invented the manner; I turned my head. That you went on living, Mr. Cohn, I regret to say, was no more than a marginal error. Such things may happen.""

"Lord," begged Calvin Cohn, a five-foot-six man in his late thirties, on his wet knees. "It wasn't as though I had a choice. I was at the bottom of the ocean attending to my work when the Devastation struck. Since I am still alive it would only be fair if You let me live. A new fact is a new condition. Though I deeply regret man's insult to a more worthy fate, still I would consider it a favor if You permit me to live."

""That cannot be my intent, Mr. Cohn. My anger has diminished but my patience is not endless. In the past I often forgave them their evil; but I shall not now. No Noah this time, no exceptions, righteous or otherwise. Though it hurts Me to say it, I must slay you; it is just. Yet because of my error, I will grant you time to compose yourself, make your peace. Therefore live quickly—a few deep breaths and go your way. Beyond that lies nothing for you. These are my words.""

"It says in Sanhedrin," Cohn attempted to

say, "'He who saves one life, it is as if he saved the world.'" He begged for another such favor.

""Although the world was saved it could not save itself. I will not save it again. I am not a tribal God; I am Master of the Universe. That means more interrelated responsibilities than you can imagine.""

Cohn then asked for a miracle.

""Miracles,"" God answered, ""go only so far. Once you proclaim it, a miracle is limited. Man would need more than a miracle.""

The Lord snapped the crack in the cloud shut. He had been invisible, light from which a voice extruded; no sign of Godcrown, silverbeard, peering eye—the image in which man had sought his own. The bulbous cloud sailed imperiously away, vanishing.

A dark coldness descended. Either the dust had thickened or night had fallen. Calvin Cohn was alone, forlorn. When he raised his head the silence all but cracked his neck.

As he struggled to stand, he lifted his fist at the darkened sky. "God made us who we are."

He danced in a shower of rocks; but that may have been his imagining. Yet those that hit the head hurt.

Cohn fell to his knees, fearing God's wrath. His teeth chattered; he shivered as though touched on the neck by icy fingers. Taking back his angry words, he spoke these: "I am not a secularist although I have doubts. Einstein said God doesn't dice with the universe; if he could believe it maybe I can. I accept Your conditions, but please don't cut my time too short."

The rusty, battered vessel with one broken mast drifted on slanted seas. Of all men only Calvin Cohn lived on, passionate to survive.

Not long after dawn, a faded rainbow appeared in the soiled sky. Although a wedge-shaped section of its arch seemed broken off, as though a triangular mouth had taken a colorful bite, Cohn wept yet rejoiced. It seemed a good sign and he needed one.

The oceanographic vessel *Rebekah Q*, a renovated iron-hulled, diesel-powered, two-masted schooner, of whose broad-sailed masts one remained erect, drifted unsteadily on the water as the Flood abated—the man-made Flood, Cohn had been instructed, not God-given.

The waters receded. They had risen high enough to overwhelm the remnants of the human race; now were slowly ebbing. He imagined the stricken vessel floating over graveyards of intricate-spired drowned cities—Calcutta, Tokyo; London on the water-swept British island. But he would not be surprised if they (he and the she-boat) were still drifting in the outraged Pacific, under whose angry waves he had sat in a small deep-sea submersible, observing the sea floor at the instant the ocean flared, and shuddered, and steamed; as nuclear havoc struck, causing a mountainous tidal wave that swallowed and spewed forth the low-lying, rusty-hulled research schooner.

Shortly thereafter Cohn had risen from the sea.

His scientist colleagues—he pictured in particular Dr. Walther Bünder departing hastily with his previously packed suitcase, his Cuban stogie clamped in his teeth—and the officers and crew who administered the ship had, seemingly without grace or goodness, disappeared. Their disregard of Cohn had outraged him, though he now admitted that in leaving him behind they had preserved him.

He had descended to the bottom of the sea twenty minutes before the missiles began to fly at each other; and when he rose from the ocean floor, the instant, totally catastrophic war had ended, and mankind had destroyed itself. The lifeboats and most of the life jackets were gone—a few left strewn on the deck. Cohn found a yellow rubber raft that had been inflated and left as though for him; he therefore forgave them their panic-stricken desertion.

He had dangled in the swaying submersible it seemed for hours after the PERIL light had flashed and the buzzer raucously signaled ASCEND. The little submarine swung in insane sweeping arcs. Its pendulous motion churned his stomach and filled it with terror until he felt the steam-powered winch begin to draw him up slowly, stopping several minutes, then drawing him up.

It was a frightful ascent. He watched thousands of maddened fish banging their blind mouths against his lit window. Cohn snapped off the lamp as the submersible moved up luminously in the watery blackness. When he reached the deck on the surface of the sea, no one appeared to secure the tiny submarine and help him out. He had bobbed around in the frothy waves, trying to escape, hopelessly seasick, before he was able to emerge from the hatch and plop, as he vomited, into the water.

Cohn pulled himself up the metal ladder on the hull of the *Rebekah Q*. The four lifeboats were gone, their ropes dangling like spaghetti strings. The sky was smeared with ashes and the reflection of flames. The ocean was thick with channels of fish scum and floating animal bodies. When the smell of dead fish assailed him, Cohn at last knew what had happened. He felt sick horror and a retching contempt of the human race. Dozens of steel missiles had plunged to the bottom of the sea and lay there like smoking turds.

Why he had survived Cohn could not guess. He had no idea how long he might go on. It seemed useless to take a radiation reading.

Some had lived after Hiroshima; some had not. What comes will come.

In the communications cabin he read a scribbled message on a warped piece of cardboard. Cohn learned what he already knew: Humanity had done itself in.

The rainbow, he remembered, was God's sign to Noah that He would not pour another deluge on the earth. So much for signs, for Covenants.

Dead souls floated on stagnant seas. The *Rebekah Q* drifted through shoals of rotting fish, and plowed through blackened seaweed in lakes of sludge.

The oceanographic schooner, its lightning-split mast draped in fallen sails, drifted close to volcanic shores as Cohn slept the heavy-hearted sleep of the dead. It sailed away from the soaking land before he woke.

He awoke mourning human beings, human existence, all the lives lost. He listed everyone he could remember, and the names of those he did not know whose names he had heard. He mourned civilization, goodness, daring, joy; and all that man had done well.

Cohn was enraged with God Who had destroyed His own dream. The war was man's; the Flood, God's. Cohn heard thunder when he thought of God and sometimes hid.

The sky was old—how often had the earth changed as the same sky looked on? Never had there been so much space in space. He had never been so desolate.

Cohn diligently pasted stamps in albums, recalling nations lost; he pitched darts at a red-and-white target in the games room. He read till his eyes were blobs of glue stuck to words. He listened to records on his father the rabbi's portable phonograph. He kept, so to speak, going.

The boat's engines had ceased throbbing; there was no electricity. It seemed useless to attempt to activate the rusty generator aboard; but there was bottled gas to cook with in the galley.

On good days Cohn told himself stories, saying the Lord would let him live if he spoke the right words. Or lived the right life. But how was that possible without another human life around? Only God and he "contending," Cohn attempting to evade His difficult nature?

(Thunder groaning, Cohn hiding.)

No way of outdoing the Lord Who had invented Himself into being. The God of beginnings; He wanted to begin, therefore had begun. Spontaneous combustion? Beginnings were far up the line from First Causes. Therefore where had God begun?

Who was He? You had to see His face to say in Whose image man had been fashioned; and no one could. Moses, who had come close, saw Him through fog and flame. Or from a cleft in a huge rock where the Lord had placed him. And God, approaching the rock in his own light, covered the cleft with His hand, until He had passed by, then removed His hand and Moses clearly saw the Lord's endless back.

Shall I someday see His face? God seemed to feel the need to talk to men. He needed worship, and even faithless men had hungered to worship Him.

Cohn added up columns of random figures. He began and tore up a notebook journal. He trotted back and forth, for exercise, along the 152-foot deck, hurdling obstacles, the fallen mast, yards of canvas sail, instruments of observation, hauling, drilling; tons of thick ropes covered with seaweed, barnacles, starfish, sea detritus; Cohn, despite his small size and slightly bowed legs, had once been an athlete in Staten Island High School.

The radio was dead. He talked to himself. He missed the human voice.

"What can one expect in this life of desolation?"

—More life?

"To be alive alone forever?"

—It takes one rib to make an Eve.

"Do you see yourself as Adam?"

—If the job is open.

Wherever they were it rarely rained. The heavy rains had served, and were gone; the present weather was dry, the flood subsiding; but not Cohn's anger at the destruction God had wrought. Why does human life mean so little to Him? Because He hadn't lived it? If Jesus had, why didn't he tell Him about it? Cohn thought he would bring Them to the bar of justice if he could.

(Terrible thundering; he hid for days.)

Drinking water was short. Part of the storage tankful had leaked into the sea, adding to the ocean water. To the bitter salt sea. Food was plentiful but he ate without appetite.

Cohn, proficient in reading geological and biological time in the microfossilized cores drilled out of the ocean floor, could barely read the visible stars. He did not know how to navigate, and could only guess where in the wet world he was; nor could he steer *Rebekah Q*, though he diligently studied repair manuals of the ship's machinery and electric system. What difference did steering make if there was no dry place to go? He went where the crippled vessel bore him, wondering whether to swim if it sank.

One tedious, sultry day Cohn thought he was no longer in the Pacific. He couldn't imagine where he was. What shall I do, alone of all men on this devastated earth?

He swore he would live on despite the wrathful God who had let him out on a string and would snap him back on a string.

Once he heard an awesome whirring of wings, and when Cohn gazed up to behold a resplendent angel, he saw a piece of torn blue sky shaped like a shrunken hand.

Cohn prayed on his knees. No voice spoke. No wind blew.

One moonlit night, Calvin Cohn, shivering in his sleep, sensed a presence aboard, surely not himself. He sat up, thinking of his dead young wife. She had been driving, not Cohn. He mourned her among those he mourned.

He feared that God, in His butcher's hat, was about to knock on the door. For the ultimate reason: ""Kiddo, it's time,"" or hinting, perhaps, to prepare Cohn? He was to be slain, God had said, though not executed. Why, therefore, hadn't it happened in his sleep rather than out of it? You go to bed and wake up dead. Or was Cohn making much of nothing real, letting fear touch his throat?

Or was this sense of another presence no more than anticipation of the land in the abated floodwaters; dove bearing in its beak a twig of olive leaf? Or raven croaking, "Land ahoy! Get your pants on"?

Cohn stared out the porthole glass; moonlight flowing on the night-calm smooth sea. No other sight.

Before reclining in his berth he drew on his green-and-blue striped sneakers and, taking along his flashlight, peeked into each cabin and lab room below the foredeck. There were creakings and crackings as he prowled from one damp room to another; but no visitors or visitations.

* * *

He woke at the sound of a whimper, switched on his torch, and strained to hear.

Cohn imagined it might be some broken thing creakily swaying back and forth in the night breeze, but it sounded like a mewling baby nearby. There had been none such aboard, nor baby's mother.

Holding a lit candle in his hand, Cohn laid his ear against each cabin door. Might it be a cat? He hadn't encountered one on the boat. Was it, then, no more than a cry in a dream?

As he was standing in his cabin, a scream in the distance shook him. Bird screeching at ship approaching shore? Impossible—there were no living birds. In Genesis, God, at the time of the First Flood, had destroyed every living thing, had burned, drowned, or starved them, except those spared on the Ark. Yet if Cohn was alive so might a single bird or mouse be.

In the morning he posted a message on the bulletin board in the games room. "Whoever you may be, kindly contact Calvin Cohn in A-11. No harm will befall you."

Afterwards, he heated up a pot of water on the gas stove and then and there gave up shaving. All supplies were short. Cohn piped out the fresh water that remained in the leaky storage tank he had unsuccessfully soldered, and let it pour into a wooden barrel he had found in the scullery. By nightfall almost an eighth of the water in the barrel was gone. That was no bird.

Who would have drunk it? Cohn feared the question as much as any response. He nailed three boards over the head of the barrel. When he wanted to drink he pried one up, then nailed it down again.

He was edgy in the galley as he scrambled a panful of powdered eggs that evening before dark, sensing he was being watched. A human eye? Cohn's skin crawled. But he had been informed by an Unimpeachable Source that he was the one man left in the world, so he persuaded himself to be calm. Cohn ate his eggs with a stale bun, washing the food down with sips of water. He was reflecting on the pleasures of a cigarette when he wondered if he had detected a slight movement of the cabinet door under the galley double-sink.

Who would that be?

The question frightened him. Cohn looked around for a cleaver and settled on a long cooking fork hanging on the wall. Holding the instrument poised like a dagger, he strode forward and pulled open the metal door.

The shriek of an animal sent his heart into flight. Cohn considered pursuing it in space but took an impulsive look inside the under-sink cabinet and could not believe what he beheld—a small chimpanzee with glowing, frightened eyes, sitting scrunched up amid bottles of cleaning fluid, grinning sickly as he clucked hoo-hoos. He wore a frayed cheesecloth compress around his neck.

"Who are you?" Cohn cried, moved by his question—that he was asking it of another living being. A live chimp-child, second small error by God Himself? The Universal Machine, off by a split cosmi-second, allows a young ape also to survive?

That being so, the realm of possibility had expanded. Cohn's mood improved. He felt more the old Cohn.

The chimp, swatting aside the cooking fork, bolted out of the cabinet, scampering forward on all fours to a swing-door that wouldn't budge. Scooting behind a tin-top work table, he climbed up a wall of shelves and sat perched at the top, persistently hooting. The chimp chattered like an auctioneer encouraging bids as he awaited Cohn's next move. At the same time he seemed to be eloquently orating: he had his rights, let him be.

Cohn kept his distance. He guessed the chimp had belonged to Dr. Walther Bünder, had heard the scientist kept one in his cabin; but Cohn had never seen the animal and forgot it existed. He had heard the doctor walked it on the deck late at night, and the little chimp peed in the ocean.

The ape on the shelf seemed to be signaling something—he tapped his toothy mouth with his fingers. The message was clear—Cohn offered him what was left of his own glass of water. Accepting it, the chimp drank hungrily. He wiped the inside of the glass with his long finger and sucked the juice before tossing the tumbler to Cohn. Hooting for attention, he tapped his mouth again, but Cohn advised him no more water till bedtime.

They were communicating!

Sitting on a kitchen stool, Calvin Cohn carefully observed the young chimpanzee, who guardedly returned his observation. He gave the impression that he was not above serious reflection, a quite intelligent animal. Descending the shelves, he self-consciously knuckle-walked toward Cohn, nervously chattering as the other sat motionless watching him.

Then the little animal mounted Cohn's lap and attempted to suckle him through his T-shirt, but he, embarrassed, fended him off. "Behave yourself." The chimp sat grooming his belly as if he had lived forever on Cohn's lap and punctually paid the rent.

He was a bowlegged, bright little boy with an expressive, affectionate face, now that his fear of Cohn seemed to have diminished. He weighed about seventy pounds, a large-craniumed creature with big ears, a flat nose, and bony-ridged curious dark eyes. His shaggy coat was brown. He seemed lively, optimistic, objective; did not say all he knew. He sat in Cohn's lap as though signifying he had long ago met, and did not necessarily despise, the human race. When in his exploration of his body hair he came on a tasty morsel, he ate it with interest. One such tidbit he offered Cohn, who respectfully declined.

He, feeling an amicable need to confide in somebody, told the little ape they had both been abandoned on this crippled ship, to an unknown fate.

At that the chimp beat his chest with the fist of one pink-palmed hand, and Cohn wondered at the response; protest, mourning—both? Whatever he meant meant meaning, comprehension. The thought of cultivating that aptitude in the animal pleased the man.

What would you tell me if you could?

The young chimp's stomach rumbled. Hopping off Cohn's lap, he reached for his hand, and tugging as he knuckle-walked, led him to a cabin in the foredeck, about thirty feet up the passage from Cohn's.

Cohn had cleaned up and dried his own room; this was a soggy mess. Scattered over the floor were pieces of a man's wearing apparel, silk shirts, striped jockey shorts, knee-length black socks, and dozens of blurred typewritten pages of what might have been a book in progress adhering to the waterlogged green rug. Among the clothes lay several damp notebooks, a damaged microscope, two rusted surgical instruments. Many swollen-paged damp books were strewn over the floor. Cohn, out of respect, placed them in the bookcase shelves, assisted by the chimp, who seemed to like doing what Cohn did. Several of the books dealt with modern and prehistoric apes; one was a fat textbook on the great apes, by Dr. Bünder. The subject of others was paleoichthyology.

As he inspected the framed pictures on the white walls, Cohn came upon a mottled color photograph of Walther Bünder, a round-faced man with a rectilinear view of life. Wearing a hard straw hat, the famous scientist sat in an armchair holding a baby chimp in diapers, recognizably the lad now standing by Cohn's side. In the photograph the baby chimp wore a small silver crucifix on a thin chain around his neck. Cohn wondered what the doctor supposed it meant to the little ape. He then tried peeking under the boy's bandage, but the chimp pushed his hand away. When Cohn was a child his mother wrapped a compress around his neck whenever his tonsils were swollen.

Cohn had talked to Dr. Bünder rarely, because he was not an accessible person. Yet once into conversation he reacted amiably, though he complained how little people had to say to each other. He had been a student of Konrad Lorenz and had written a classic text on the great apes before concerning himself with prehistoric fish. He said he had divorced his wife because she had produced three daughters and never a son. "She did not look to my needs." He argued she was just as responsible as he for the sex-type of their children. And he had not remarried because he did not "in ezzence" trust women. He called himself a natural philosopher.

Cohn "had to say" that he had studied for the rabbinate, but was not moved by his calling—as he was by his father's calling—so he had become instead a paleologist. The doctor offered Cohn a Cuban cigar he had imported from Zurich.

Why the doctor had not taken his little chimp with him at the very end, Cohn couldn't say, unless the chimpanzee had hidden in panic when the alarm bells rang, and could not be located by his master. Or the doctor, out of fear for his own life, had abandoned his little boy.

What's his loss may be my gain, Cohn reflected.

Close by Dr. Bünder's berth stood a barred, wooden holding cage four feet high. In it lay a small, damp Oriental rug and two rusted tin platters. The chimp, as though to demonstrate the good life he had lived, stepped into the cage, swinging the door shut, and then impulsively snapped the lock that had been hanging open on the hasp. A moment later he gazed at Cohn in embarrassed surprise, as though he had, indeed, done something stupid. Seizing the wooden bars with both hands, he fiercely rattled them.

Get me out of here.

"Think first," Cohn advised him.

Cohn went through the doctor's pockets, in his wet garments, but could not find a key to the cage. He pantomimed he would have to break the door in.

The chimp rose upright, displaying; he swaggered from foot to foot. It did him no good, so he tried sign language, but Cohn shook his head—he did not comprehend. The animal angrily orated; this was his home and he loved it.

"Either I bang the door in, or you stay there for the rest of your natural life," Cohn told him.

The chimpanzee kicked at the cage and grunted in pain. He held his foot to show where it hurt.

Cohn, for the first time since the Day of Devastation, laughed heartily.

The little chimp chattered as if begging for a fast favor, but Cohn aimed his boot at the locked wooden door and bashed it in.

The chimp, his shaggy hair bristling, charged out of the cage, caught Cohn's right thumb between his canines and bit.

Cohn, responding with a hoarse cry, slapped his face—at once regretting it. But it ended there because, although his thumb bled, he apologized.

The ape presented his rump to Cohn, who instinctively patted it. He seemed to signal he would like to do the same for Cohn, and he presented his right buttock and was touched by the animal. Civilized, Cohn thought.

* * *

In one of the damp notebooks whose pages had to be carefully teased apart, the writing barely legible because the purple fountain-pen ink had run—not to speak of the doctor's difficult Gothic script—was his record of the little ape's progress in learning the Ameslan sign language for the deaf. "He knows already all the important signs. He mages egzellent progress." The accent played in Cohn's head as he read the doctor's words. He could hear him mumbling to himself as he scratched out his sentences.

Calvin Cohn searched for a list of illustrated language signs but could not find them. Trying another soggy notebook, he came across additional entries concerning Dr. Bünder's experiment in teaching the boy to speak with him. On the last page he found a note in the scientist's tormented handwriting to the effect that he was becoming bored with the sign-language exercises, "although Gottlob gobbles it up. I must try something more daring. I think he ist now ready for it. He ist quite a fellow."

Gottlob!

That was the last entry in this notebook, dated a week before the Day of Devastation.

Cohn was not fond of the name Dr. Bünder had hung on the unsuspecting chimp; it did not seem true to type, flapped loose in the breeze. Was he patronizing his boy or attempting to convert him? Leading the ape by his hairy hand to his cabin, Cohn got out his old Pentateuch, his Torah in Hebrew and English which he had recently baked out in the hot sun, flipped open a wrinkled page at random and put his finger on it. He then informed the little chimp that he now had a more fitting name, one that went harmoniously with the self he presented. In other words he was Buz.

Cohn told him that Buz was one of the descendants of Nahor, the brother of Abraham the Patriarch, therefore a name of sterling worth and a more suitable one than the doctor had imposed on him.

To his surprise the chimp seemed to disagree. He reacted in anger, beat his chest, jumped up and down in breathy protest. Buz was obviously temperamental.

But his nature was essentially unspoiled. Since his objections had done him no great good, he moodily yawned and climbed up on the top berth where, after counting his fingers and toes, he fell soundly asleep on his back.

His mouth twitched in sleep and his eye movements indicated he was dreaming. Somebody he was hitting on the head with a rock? Except that his expression was innocent.

Cohn felt they could become fast friends, possibly like brothers.

Who else do I have?

He locked Buz in the doctor's cabin, and

let him out in the morning to have breakfast with him in the galley.

Cohn observed that the chimp had done his business in his tin dish in the cage. Clever fellow, he suited himself to circumstance. Afterwards they played hide-and-seek and Cohn swung him in circles by his long skinny arms on the sunny, slightly listing deck. Buz shut his eyes and opened his mouth as he sailed through the air.

Cohn enjoyed playing with him but worried about diminishing food supplies. Canned goods, except for five cases of sardines, twelve of vegetarian baked beans and three of tuna fish, plus two cases of sliced peach halves in heavy syrup, were about gone; but there was plenty of rice and flour in large bins. The frightening thing was the disappearing drinking water. There were only a few gallons in the barrel. Cohn doled it out a tablespoon at a time.

What if they went on drifting on the vast ocean without ever landing? The worst was yet to come. Wait till God discovered His second little error—that Buz, too, had momentarily escaped his final fate. Not that he was alive when he shouldn't be, but that he hadn't expired when he was supposed to. Or had He already discovered it and was making plans? The Lord was mysterious. His speech was silence, His presence, mystery. He made life a mystery, problematic for anyone attempting to survive.

In a week the water supply was all but depleted. Cohn considered attempting to distill sea water but hadn't the equipment. Besides, the gas was low. Simply cooking salt water all day and trying to collect its steam would be an impossible task. Still, if they had to they would try.

If only it would rain again, no deluge, just enough to store up some precious water. Maybe he oughtn't to have kept Buz on ship, who ate as though starved, and if given a chance drank twice as much water as Cohn. Ought he to have kicked the ape overboard? Should he—to preserve himself? Could he?

As he was contemplating desperate measures, the sky darkened. Cohn lugged up on deck the all-but-empty water barrel, and Buz carried up a copper frying pan he had found below. He banged the clattering instrument as though summoning a rain God.

And as if the rain God had himself appeared, the wind rose with a wail and in minutes the black, thickened sky poured water on water. The rising waves lifted the battered schooner on swelling seas, then dropped it low. Now the rudderless vessel plunged through fierce, roiling currents, driven southward by the hurricane.

A howling wind raged. Cohn had tightly tied the ashen-faced chimpanzee to the broken mast, as the *Rebekah Q* dipped and rose, from ocean pit to sky, in the hissing waves. They watched the storm with shut eyes, the drenched little chimp whimpering after he had thrown up.

Cohn, shivering within himself, feared they'd be washed into the heaving sea. Drowning would be the end of it, the last wet page of life. Today may be the day He slays us, though why does He complicate it so when He can knock us off with one small lightning bolt? Mission completed, the earth cleansed of living creatures, except maybe an underweight cockroach under a wooden sink in Bombay, that He will knock off with His spray gun the next time it exposes its frantic antennaed head. What makes Him so theatrical? Cohn wondered. He enjoys performance, spectacle—people in peril His most entertaining circus. He loves sad stories, with casts of thousands. Cohn hid his anger at The Lord, turning it low, then hid his thoughts.

After hours of anguished enduring, Calvin Cohn watched the slow night unfold as the wind gently subsided. The sea grew quiet, the storm abated. A white star hung like a lucent pearl in the clearing sky. The chimp had revived and was listening with interest to his borborygmus. Any voice interested him. They had sailed southeast after south and were not drifting north-northeast. Cohn guessed they had voyaged out of the Pacific, but where in the world are we?

In the morning the sun blazed like a flaming bronze mirror. Cohn untied himself and Buz, whereupon the little chimp embraced him in his hairy arms. And they kissed. In his expressive mood Buz inserted two fingers under his neck cloth and tugged at something; he handed Cohn a small silver cross on a broken chain, perhaps as a gift.

One God is sufficient, thought Cohn. But instead of casting it into the water he slipped it into his pocket.

The chimp hastily rehearsed his repertoire of language signs, none of which Cohn knew, though he was able to guess out a couple of the more obvious ones. And the barrel on the deck was brimming with rainwater, slightly salted. It seemed as though the ship itself sought the end of its voyage but had trouble arriving upon it.

The sinking boat was leaking through its rusty hull. If they lasted one more day he'd be surprised. And where was land? As if to say *look!* two violet-blue jacaranda blossoms appeared on the lavender water, trailed by a palm frond and two green-leaved bamboo shoots.

And he spied four dead rainbow fish; had assumed they were alive until he shook out the bottom of a paper bag of bread crumbs on the glazed water. The fish did not flicker. The air was heavily humid. Cohn focused his binoculars into the hazy distance and saw moving fog. No birds present, not an albatross or pelican, or anything smaller.

He inspected their yellow rubber raft and gathered supplies and objects of craft and art to take ashore, granting they arrived at a shore. He collected several precious books, and the water in ten-gallon jugs. Cohn had hand-picked, from cabin to cabin, piles of clothing for all seasons; all the provisions he could carry; also a portable wind-up phonograph with a dozen uncracked records, seventy-eights, long ago the property of his father the rabbi who had once been a cantor; plus yards of lumber and a full tool chest, with gimlets and awls. And he took with him a small off-white urn containing his pregnant wife's ashes. She had been cremated before the universal cremation, her will, not Cohn's; she had seemed always to know what was coming next.

That night, while Buz and Cohn were asleep in their upper and lower beds, the vessel shuddered, splintered, and cracked stupendously as it went grindingly aground. The chimp was pitched out of his berth and began to hoot in the dark; but Cohn got a candle lit and calmed him, saying they would no longer be at the mercy of a foundering ship.

At dawn Buz slid down a rope as Cohn climbed down the tilted ship's ladder, stepping on the blackened surface of a coral reef on whose algae-covered mass the *Rebekah Q,* jaggedly broken in two, was pulled up tight. Across a narrow channel lay a strip of coastal land, possibly an island.

Buz stepped into the water, and to Cohn's great surprise, began swimming across the channel to the verdant thick-treed shore. A chimp paddling on his back? A genius chimp, Cohn reflected.

They'd be like brothers, if not father and son.

Arriving on shore, the dripping ape thumbed his comic nose at Cohn, and sauntering forward, plunged into the steaming rain forest without so much as a glance backward.

Hours later, having brought in the yellow raft laden with supplies to the green shore, then hidden them in the saw-toothed tall grass, an exhausted Cohn followed Buz into the forest. He figured God had, at long length, permitted him to go on living, otherwise He wouldn't have let Cohn leave the wrecked vessel and make for shore.

The Lord, baruch Ha-shem, had moved from His Judgment to His Mercy seat. Cohn would fast. Today must be Yom Kippur.

Cohn's Island

His first night on the island—the massive silence was unreal—Cohn spent in a scarlet-blossomed candelabrum tree, although there were no wild beasts to hide from. In the rain forest no birds sang or insects buzzed; no snakes slithered on their bellies; no moths, bats, or lizards had survived. No friend Buz, for that matter; Cohn had seen no sign of the young ape. How desolate the world was; how bleak experience, when only one experienced.

Where were the dead? He had come across yards of scattered bones. None were fossils. All were skeletons of animals that had perished in the Devastation, among them an undersize leopard and a lady chimpanzee. He found no bones of men, felt a renewal of abandonment, but kept himself busy exploring the island.

In the morning he discovered—there where the rain forest curved behind a rocky, hilly area, and flowed north—several caves in a striated yellow sandstone escarpment, and Cohn chose the largest, a double-caverned chamber, to shelter himself. The escarpment, as high as a five-story tenement backed against a parapet of green and lilac hills, was a many-ledged bluff topped by masses of wild ferns, mossy epiphytic saplings, and cord-thick vines dripping down its face.

Cohn ascended the escarpment, practically a walk-up. From a terraced enclosure like a small balcony two-thirds of the way up, he paused for a view of the woodsy neighborhood—the rain forest, a wall of steaming vegetation in the west moving north; and toward east a sparser woodland of flowering trees and thick-grassed fields extending to the southern shore of the island, lined with varieties of wild palm.

From the left side of the escarpment, which looked like a fortress from the shore, a waterfall resembling a horse's bushy tail fell, forming a foaming pool where it hit the rocky ground. The pool overflowed into a downward sloping savanna, beyond which the rain forest grew over a section of hills to the northern sea, where Cohn and Buz had landed on a coral reef.

After this initially unsettling yet engrossing view of his domain, Cohn's disposition improved.

He set to work diligently clearing the anterior, and smaller, of the two caves, carrying out shovel loads of black mud; he tore out armfuls of entangled dead vines; and hauled buckets of rocks and wet sand. Cohn unearthed two stone ledges, one along the rear of the cave where it opened into the larger cavern; the other an almost rounded table of sandstone extending from the left wall as one entered the cave, an all-purpose work platform on which he figured he would prepare food, assemble and repair objects he might need; and on which he could build cooking fires.

The cave, surely eighteen feet high, ten broad, and twenty feet deep, showed no high-water line of the Flood. That appeared on the face of the escarpment about thirty feet up. Despite the humid heat Cohn lit a fire to bake out the cave. He had dragged in a quantity of lumber, transported with great difficulty from the reef—a pile of boards of mixed woods and lengths that he managed to fit under the long rock ledge; and in a week he set to work constructing a wall of shelves ten feet by twelve high and wide, and two deep, where he stored his possessions, such as they were, and would keep whatever else he might collect. It occurred to Cohn he seemed to be assuming a future, for better or worse.

Using the fine tools he had carted along from the oceanographic vessel, which included a surveyor's telescope, he built himself a rough small table, sturdy cot, and a primitive rocker with water-barrel staves; then Cohn constructed an outside hut not far from a small stand of white acacia trees about thirty feet from the cave. The hut was walled with split saplings on three sides, and the fourth was left open because he liked to look at a grassy, wooded area that sloped to the sea.

His hut was covered with a bamboo roof insulated from the heat by a thatch of palm fronds interwoven with strips of bark. When Cohn tired of the cave—his bedroom, kitchen, and living area—he sat in the hut, more like an open porch and revery room. There he had strung up a canvas hammock he had made from a sail, where he often lay, reflecting on his lonely fate.

Can I call this a life?

Better than death.

Why bother?

"Because I breathe."

When the humidity grew intolerable he rested in the cool cave, lit at night by a kerosene lamp. He considered constructing a gate across the oval opening, but why get involved if there were no inconvenient animals around? And gate or no gate the Lord knew where he lived, if He felt like dropping in to talk with His little mistake.

* * *

A week or two after his arrival on the island Cohn was struck by a nauseating illness, felt ghastly, headachy to the pits of his eyes, shivered feverishly. He vomited continuously though he ate nothing to vomit. Cohn sweated; he stank. He lost hair in dreadful quantities; it fell from his head as he lay on the floor on an old overcoat. He lost his short brown beard, chest and pubic hair, every bit on his body.

Cohn guessed he was afflicted by radiation poisoning, or had been affected—perhaps in addition—by excessive bursts of X-rays trespassing in the shredded ozone. Is it the Swiss-cheese ozone or the will of God that makes me ill? Maybe He knows I'm still angry at Him? Cohn thought he had better watch his thoughts. He who knoweth the voice of the bird way up there isn't above knowing what C. Cohn thinks. I'd better stay out of His ESP and/or Knowing Eye. But sick as I am I won't knock on His perilous door, even if I knew where it is. Let Him look me up if He's in the mood for instant benediction.

Cohn doctored himself as best he could, with aspirin and sips of stale water. To coat his stomach he chewed grains of raw rice, though it did no apparent good. He vomited anything he imbibed; fouled himself disgracefully; felt abandoned, outcast, bleak. Nobody was present to cluck in sympathy at poor Cohn's fate. He could not stand very much more of the same. ""Live quickly,"" the Lord had said. ""A few deep breaths and go your way."" Calvin Cohn, as though in agreement, slipped out of consciousness of the world it was.

During a long night of delirium, with morbid intervals of awareness and no desire to go on, cursing the woman who had given him birth and anybody who had assisted in the enterprise, Cohn woke in the drafty front cave to the sensuous presence (Mama forgive me) of a hand lifting his aching head. It then seemed to the sick man that a delicious elixir of coconut was flowing down his parched throat.

In the glowing dark he was teased by a thought that he was being assisted and fed by a heavy-breathing, grunting, black god, holding half a fragrant coconut to his wasted lips as Cohn gulped; or was he still delirious and the experience illusion, dreamthought?

"Buz?" he murmured and got no response. Cohn reached forth to touch the god, if god it was, or beast; a hand withdrew and his head struck the ground. The pain, flashing a dozen lightnings, confused him.

In the morning two ripe red bananas lay by his side, and with them four soft oranges. Cohn reached for one, cupping it in his gaunt hands, deeply breathing its orange fragrance as the warm fumes rose in his head. He bit the skin and sucked the fruit dry. Going by this statement of his senses, Cohn lived on. He had one constant dream: he was alone in the world if not elsewhere.

His nausea returned but not the creature (or whoever) that had fed him. Cohn, still seriously ill, heaved up the fruity contents of his stomach and sank into a coma. How long it endured he didn't know. Or whether he had had a visitor or visitors. When he came out of it, he could not separate experience from what might have been. Anyway, here was Cohn lying on the warm ground in bright sun, in open view of the cloudless island sky. Whoever-he-was had dragged or carried him in his soiled overcoat out of the cave into the grass before his hut, where the acacias grew at the edge of the woods and field that led to the sea.

For days it seemed to Cohn he lay there barely able to stir, staring at the sky, hoping to recover health and existence. Whoever-his-protector continued to provide fruit of several sorts, plus acacia leaves for decoration--and as of yesterday, washed rootstocks of cassava. Cohn, having nothing else to occupy him, forced himself to chew the bitter, starchy root, sensing it nourished him. He had lost a great deal of weight and was afraid to look at any part of himself. But he felt a hot breeze wander over him, indicating he had substance; and when Cohn touched his head to see if it was still there, he could feel a growing fluff of hair. Fortunately it rarely rained as he lay outside; at times drizzled.

Each day fruit and washed root appeared. If he awoke early to see who was feeding him, invariably there was no delivery. He fell asleep and when he awakened later his portion was present, together with a broken piece of sugar cane. Cohn daily thanked his benefactor but hadn't the pleasure of making his or her acquaintance.

One morning, after devouring a breakfast of five pieces of fruit, Cohn got up and dunked himself in the fresh-water pool formed by the horsetail waterfall, from which a spring flowed into the savanna beyond the side of the escarpment. Here Cohn had bathed shortly after arriving in this part of the island, as though to celebrate his arrival; and now he bathed to cleanse himself of his illness.

He dried his legs, sitting on a warm large rock in the sun, and drew on a white silk shirt of Dr. Bünder's, his own denims, and blue-and-green sneakers. Cohn liked being dressed; Adam probably had got to enjoy his fig leaf.

Afterwards Calvin Cohn sat in his rocker in the open but couldn't work up energy to read. He shut his eyes and was dreaming of sleep when he heard a rustle in one of the white-flowered acacias. Glancing up, he saw to his happy surprise Buz himself sitting on a low bough, paying no attention to his former friend and mentor. He was eating a small, wrinkled, plum-like fruit with a greenish center. Cohn, an old encyclopedia hand, recognized it as passion fruit. Buz held four bunched in his pink palm. He still wore his decaying neck cloth as though out of affection. His supple toes held to the tree limb. The chimp's phallus and fleshy scrotum were visible, a more than respectable apparatus for a boy his age.

When Buz saw Cohn observing him he let out an instinctive squawk and chattered angrily at the fuzzy creature below; then, as if recognition had lit a lamp, hooted conversationally. Cohn spoke a few words of welcome home, refraining from mentioning the ape's desertion of him or engaging in a complaint of his recent woes.

He had noticed that Buz's shaggy coat adorned him in tufts and patches, and that the hair on his head had thinned out and left him slightly bald. He wasn't as skinny as Cohn but had obviously been ill.

Buz, in courteous acknowledgment of Cohn's greetings, tossed down one of his passion fruits; it struck him on the head, and though it was a pitless fruit, knocked him cold. The ape, after eating those he held in his palm, curiously inspected Cohn's supine body and at last climbed down to attend him.

Cohn said Kaddish for one hundred souls whose names he had picked at random in a heavily thumbed copy of a Manhattan telephone directory he had snatched from the sea-battered *Rebekah Q*. He kept it for company in the cave as a sort of "Book of the Dead."

He often felt an urge to read all those names aloud. The Dead must be acknowledged if one respected life. He would say Kaddish at least once for everyone in the book, although, technically speaking, to do so one needed the presence of ten live Jews. Yet, since there were not ten in the world, there was no sin saying it via only one man. Who was counting?

God said nothing.

Cohn said Kaddish.

There's a legend in Midrash that Moses did not want to die despite his so-called old age. He was against it, respectfully, of course.

"Master of the World! Let me stay like a bird that flies on the four winds and gathers its food every day, and at eventide returns to the nest. Let me be like one of them!"

""With all due regard for services rendered,"" God said, ""nothing doing. You're asking too much. That mixes everything up. First things first.""

Cohn said Kaddish.

If we were bound to come to this dreadful end, why did the All-knowing God create us?

Some sages said: In order to reflect His light. He liked to know He was present.

Some said: In order to create justice on earth; at least to give it a try.

Cohn thought: He was the Author of the universe. Each man was a story unto himself, it seemed. He liked beginnings and endings. He enjoyed endings based on beginnings, and beginnings on endings. He liked to guess out endings and watch them go awry. At first He liked the juicy parts where people were torn between good and evil; but later the stories may have let Him down: how often, without seeming to try, the evil triumphed. It wasn't an effect; it was an embarrassing condition: His insufficient creation. Man was subtly conceived but less well executed. Body and soul hung badly together.

Maybe next time.

Cohn said Kaddish.

When he recovered from his radiation illness, he had acquired a light-brown beard and slim, tanned body, but his short legs, from childhood a bit bent, seemed more so. No cows, no calcium. One day he journeyed with Buz by rubber raft to the coral atoll on the northwestern side of the island to see what they might recover from the wreck of *Rebekah Q*. Many useful objects were too large for transportation by raft, but they could pile up small things, about a four-hundred-pound load each trip.

The cave was a sloping half mile from the southern shore of the island, on the opposite side from the reefs; and it was best to carry in supplies by raft around the island rather than attempt to lug them through the rain forest by tortuous, all-but-impossible routes. Cohn had made five trips to the beached boat, before he became ill, and had gathered many useful objects. Given his uncertain destiny, he felt he ought not pass up any serviceable item.

He paddled at the forward-port corner, and Buz imitated his friend, wielding his aluminum oar in the starboard corner. Or if the chimp dozed off, Cohn, with difficulty, rowed alone.

A breeze had risen and the water was choppy; it took half the morning to arrive at the reef. The grounded vessel, broken in two and lying broadside the sea, was still there, sprayed by waves chopping against the bony atoll.

Cohn had previously taken back with him *The Works of William Shakespeare*, his old Pentateuch, a one-volume encyclopedia, a college dictionary, and a copy—there were eight in his cabin—of Dr. Walther Bünder's *The Great Apes*, a classic textbook containing three excellent chapters on the life cycle of the chimpanzee.

Now he set aside Morris Fishbein's *Medical Adviser, The Joys of Simple Cookery, How to do Satisfying Carpentry,* and several volumes on paleontology and geology, plus two novels that had once belonged to his wife, may she rest in peace. He had, for entertainment's sake, considered and discarded *A Manual of Sexual Skills for Singles,* found in Dr. Bünder's bottom dresser drawer.

Buz kept for himself a can opener, after he had succeeded in raggedly opening a tin of Portuguese sardines in oil, of which he ate every little fish without offering Cohn a bite.

The ape insisted on dragging along the holding cage he had inhabited and to which he was affectionately attached. They packed the raft as best they could, for fear of overloading leaving behind on the atoll four gallons of linseed oil, a large jar of vitamin C, also Cohn's portable typewriter because he doubted he would write another letter. As for a journal, if he should keep one, he preferred to do it in his handwriting.

He tried to persuade Buz to abandon his silly cage, but the chimp, hooting, on the verge of displaying anger, would not yield. After their return journey in calmer waters, Buz tugged and lugged his cage along the shore and up the long rise to the cave; and he stored it under the stone ledge where Cohn kept what was left of his lumber, a dirty-clothes basket, plus several brooms and a dust mop he had collected.

The next time they returned to the reef—on a cloudy morning after a week of rain—Cohn wondered if they had come to the wrong one, for the vessel was gone. But it was the right reef and the vessel was gone.

The oil, vitamins, and portable typewriter

had been washed away. And Cohn felt sadness at the final loss of the ship, the last home he had had in a homeless world. He forgave Buz for wanting to retain his holding cage.

To explore the island, Cohn made trips in stages by raft, and forays into the interior, hiking with Buz. The chimp's ordinary mode of locomotion was knuckle-walking, but he enjoyed brachiating, was talented at it, though no gibbon—hadn't their almost flying skills. He would, however, climb into the crown of a tall tree and fling himself forward, grasping arm-thick liana vines to hold himself aloft before dropping into the next tree. Cohn admired his skill in plunging from one to another without stopping to think about it.

In the rain forest Buz left Cohn behind, a compass in his hand, trying to hack his way out of the dense undergrowth that made hash of his clothes. Cohn wielded a fine, exquisitely sharp, French saber from the Franco-Prussian War that the chimp had discovered, and borrowed from Dr. Bünder's trunk.

The massive equatorial rain forest was canopied with interwoven branches of leaves festooned with mossy looping vines, through which sunlight barely filtered. The effect was of lit green gloom over a shadowy forest floor. Saplings smothered each other in their struggle to arrive at light.

Parts of the forest floor were covered with flowers. Cohn caught glimpses of vermilion, white, and yellow blossoms. Man and beast had expired but not flowers; the Lord loved their fragrance and color. But who were the pollinators? unless there was a little bee around—God's grace—fructifying the little flowers? How vegetation existed without insects or other small creatures to pollinate plants, Cohn didn't know but could guess: the Lord Himself had creatively taken over. Even the distorted fruits Cohn had found on many trees on his arrival had reassumed their natural forms. ““Grow,”” He said, because that was His nature. And trees and flowers blossomed and bloomed.

The Lord enjoyed beginnings and He usually began by phasing some things out—to make room. Creation soon created crowds. What was He maybe into now? A touch of life without death? Bacteria, for instance, also continued to exist. Maybe this island was Paradise, although where was everybody who had been rumored to be rentless in eternity? No visible living creature moved through the outsize vegetation, only a lone Jewish gentleman and a defenseless, orphaned chimp he had, by chance, befriended on a doomed oceanography vessel.

It took them about two weeks to encircle the island in their yellow raft, camping on land at night, eating from wild fruit trees and root patches, sucking sugar cane; and where there were no streams or waterholes, drinking fresh water Buz found in tree holes. They had begun this journey on the beach below Cohn's cave and had paddled east, then north at the highlands. The island was shaped like a broken stubby flask, it seemed to Cohn. Its bottom had split off in the recent Devastation and sunk into the sea.

On the northern coast as they paddled west, the shoreline was indented by a series of coves and short bays with coarse, sandy beaches; and where the mouth of the flask appeared, a half-dozen atolls shielded the shore.

Every so often they had drawn the raft up on the beach and commenced a fossil dig nearby for a day or so. Cohn kept extensive notes on the bones they unearthed. He was interested in bone movement. And he searched for hominids and found varieties of small ancient animals. He had discovered some surprising samples and felt he ought to knock out an article or two, if for no other reason than to keep up the habit. He wished he had saved his typewriter from the sea, the loss a result of momentary confusion. Buz enjoyed making small holes bigger and breaking rocks with Cohn's hammer. When his eye lit on an interesting bone he beckoned Cohn over to make the identification. To date they had found six teeth of Eohippus—an extraordinary find, two chimp leg bones and a gorilla jaw, possibly from Pliocene times. Also a Jurassic mouse, and an ancient giant raccoon from the Miocene epoch. It was a pretty old island.

Cohn guessed from the vegetation that it lay somewhere in what had once been the Indian Ocean, perhaps off the southern coast of old Africa, possibly over a more or less dead volcano that had bubbled up in the ocean bed. Too bad he had left behind all his diving equipment.

The island, he figured, was about twenty miles in length, and maybe six miles across, except at its midpoint where it seemed to bulge to nine or ten; and at its northeastern end, where it shrank to two across for three miles or so—the mouth of the flask.

Thinking of names, he considered calling it Broken End Island. He also thought of Chimpan Zee in honor of his young friend, and at last settled for Cohn's Island. On a narrow mid-island beach he set up a sign stating the name of the place; but when they were once more embarked on the raft Cohn had second thoughts and felt he ought to remove the sign next time around, lest the Lord accuse him of hubris.

Cohn supposed that the island had been four or five miles longer than at present. On the Day of Devastation an earthquake struck, and a portion of the highland mass split off and sank into the sea. What was left of the land had been overwhelmed by a tidal wave—the first stage of the World Flood, from which it had slowly, recently, recovered.

Perhaps the island inhabitants, in fishing and farming villages sloping down the hills, had rushed in panic to higher ground, and as they ran were swept by the tidal wave into the ocean; as were those who, in panic, had remained where they were.

Cohn, as they had rowed the raft around to the northern coast from the east, had beheld a forest of brown dead-leaved tops of trees rising in the mild waves touching the rockbound shore. He thought he could see, in the near distance, a drowned village under water.

Could the Lord see it?

The late-autumn rains—cold, pulpy raindrops—poured torrentially; and soon, in a second or third growing season, streams of small orange, pink, and huge purple flowers Cohn had never laid eyes on before sprang up on the earth.

The rain went on, with a few dry periods, from possibly October to December, and March through May—Cohn did not know because he kept no calender; his watch had stopped, he would not wind it up. It extended time not to hack it to bits and pieces. Perhaps this was closer to the Lord's duration. He was not much concerned with minutes, or hours, and after Creation, with days, except the Sabbath. His comfortable unit of existence was the universe enduring.

In the afternoon, the rain lightened and Cohn would go forth in his woolen brown poncho and rain-repellent fur hat to search for fruit.

Buz, who swam when he had to, could not stand the wet; it depressed him. When the rain was heavy he sat semi-catatonically in the cave, staring at the water streaming down. It poured as a solid sheet of wet, blurring the trees. When it let up they went forth together, and if they happened to be caught in a renewed downpour, the chimp sheltered himself under a thick-leaved tree, his hands crossed on his chest, his head bent, body hair shedding water. It was as though he mourned when it rained.

Cohn wanted to know why.

The ape hooted.

Cohn prepared a map of fruit trees with footnotes saying when and how they bore fruit. The palms yielded oil, coconuts, dates, round hard red nuts. Buz collected coconuts and carried them to the cave—four in his arms against his chest. Cohn, after tapping them open with a claw hammer, milked each and saved the juice in a jug as a refreshing drink and tasty flavoring agent. And then he hammered the coconut pulp into a delicious paste, flavored with vanilla or chocolate, that they relished as candy.

Buz led Cohn to a small grove of yellow banana trees whose plentiful fruit they ate, ripe, and sometimes fried; and that Cohn fermented in a barrel vat into a pleasant beer that Buz was fond of. When available they collected mangoes—to which Cohn had discovered he was allergic; and figs, passion fruit, oranges, but no lemons—none grew on the island—all of which, except the mangoes, he cut up and mixed with chunks of coconut and pieces of cassava into a delicious salad. He built a trap in the cold stream beyond the pool and used it as an icebox. They ate twice daily; nobody suffered hunger.

Despite the mortal insult the earth had endured, it yielded fruit and flowers, a fact that said a good word for God. Cohn had become a fructivore, except when fruit was unripe or unavailable—fortunately not for long, because they picked and stored it for reasonably lengthy periods.

When there was nothing else to eat they opened tins of sardines or tuna fish. Though the young ape relished these specialties, Cohn felt he was violating an ethic if he ate them. He had pledged himself never to ingest what had once been a living creature.

Therefore he boiled up rice, and with the flour from the ship, baked—since there was no yeast—matzo-like unleavened breadcakes on flat stones in the wood fire on the round stone ledge. The large cave acted as a ventilator, and once in a while a not always comfortable damp draft blew out of it.

Buz ate the thin, often burnt breadcakes in small portions, unable to work up an appetite for Cohn's rice and bread cookery unless he added a fistful of leaves to the collation—his little salad.

The late autumn months were a dreary time of damp and cold on the island. Cohn hadn't expected the chill. He wore long johns, wool socks, and his overcoat on two sweaters; and he permitted Buz to borrow his poncho if he wanted it. Cohn suspected that something unusual had altered the climate, perhaps ashes of the destroyed world imprisoned in winds in the atmosphere.

That meant hotter and colder than ordinary weather; and he sometimes wondered whether vegetation would continue to endure if God looked away a few celestial seconds. And whether the rain forest would turn black and expire. Cohn was concerned that a new ice age might be in the making, not usually likely on an equatorial island of this size and climatology; but the Lord had His mysterious ways and was not about to explain them.

Cohn insulated the cave as best he could, with two sacks of cement and some rocks he broke up with his hammer; he filled the opening between the caves to a height of six feet. That left space for ventilation, especially important when the wood they burned was wet and smoked heavily. But the cave was comfortable and on dry days smelled of grass; and on wet days smelled like a wet forest. For himself he had added short legs to the cot he had constructed, and made of it a bed of split saplings covered with a layer of mimosa leaves, and a canvas sheet with his overcoat as blankets.

Buz, when it wasn't raining, preferred to rest in a nearby acacia; and when it rained at night he slept in his holding cage, despite the fact that he had grown three inches since he and his friend had met. His head, when Cohn pulled him up by his hands, reached to Cohn's chest, appreciably narrower than Buz's. Though his legs were naturally bent, the chimp covered ground rapidly, sustaining his balance with ease, and propelling himself forward with his knuckles touching the ground. When they raced for fun, invariably Cohn fell behind.

They played tag, hide-and-seek, nut-in-the-hole, an aggie game he had taught him that Buz liked extraordinarily well, although he rolled his nut clumsily and Cohn often let him win by rolling his own so forcefully it shot past the hole. Victory, however arranged, made no difference to Buz so long as he won. He grunted as he ate, danced on occasion, and if Cohn tickled him, responded by tickling Cohn. Cohn enjoyed laughing helplessly—it fitted the scheme of things. And he often thought what a fine friend Buz would make if he could talk.

As spring neared, Cohn, wearing an old army cap to protect his head in the sun, worked with rocks and dead tree limbs to divert the stream that flowed from the waterfall across the savanna below the farther hills. Cohn dammed it and fed the water as irrigation to a rice paddy he had constructed after reading an article and studying a picture in his encyclopedia; and he seeded it with rice sprouts he had grown in the cave. Within about four months he harvested a crop of rice and planted another. So long as the Lord was in a genial mood there would be rice forever. Cohn played with thoughts of immortality.

He also planted—from seeds he had collected and saved—yams and black-eyed beans. Unfortunately there was no lettuce or tomatoes anywhere on the island. Cohn relished salad but could not enjoy leaf salads, passing them up when Buz arrived with his offerings. He presented him too—from his mouth into Cohn's palm—with a chewed-up green gob of leaves; but Cohn was not tempted.

Buz now and then assisted with the gardening. His fingers weren't subtle and he was inefficient in planting, when Cohn, on his insistence, let him help. Buz cupped a small mound of beans in his palm but found it difficult to insert them individually into the soft soil; so he chewed up some and flung the rest away. Cohn thought he might be of more help in harvesting.

But Buz was comparatively handy with a few tools. He liked plunging the point of his can opener into the top of a can, working it raggedly around until the tin was cut and he could get his fingers under the lid. He had learned to slice fruit with a knife and he used a hammer fairly accurately. All Cohn had to do was tap the tip of a nail into wood and Buz would drive it in all the way.

Cohn crafted things. He carved wood with a jackknife and chisel, and made bowls, platters, pitchers. He carved a variety of wooden flowers and animals for remembrance. He wove fibers of cactus into stiff little cloths he wasn't sure what to do with, and gathered and polished stones.

One day he fixed up a small hammock for Buz, converting a topcoat of Dr. Bünder's. He tied it between two live oak saplings, and Buz lay in it, swinging gently until he fell off to sleep. The chimp liked sunbathing in his hammock. He also enjoyed sniffing Cohn's bare feet as he lay in his hammock contemplating his fate.

Would He have given me Buz if He intended to slay me?

That night in the cave, Cohn said the island was shaped like a short, stubby bottle.

Buz pantomimed he disagreed, a grunt with a shake of the head. He pantomimed peeling a banana.

"A little like one, maybe," Cohn nodded, "but a lot more like a stubby bottle, in my eye."

A banana, Buz insisted.

* * *

Cohn had brought from the *Rebekah Q* five of Dr. Bünder's fairly legible, waterlogged notebooks. He had discovered in one of them approximately forty partially blurred small drawings of sign-language images the scientist had taught the chimp. Cohn practiced as many signs as he could read.

One day, as he sat in his rocker with Buz on his lap, he signaled to the chimp: "We—you and I—are alone in this world. Do you understand?"

The chimp signaled, "Buz wants fruit."

Cohn signed: "I feel alone (lonely). Is Buz lonely?"

The chimp signed, "What is alone?"

Cohn, excited by the ape's genuine question, pantomimed signs that might mean sad, unhappy, oppressed.

Buz signed, "Play with Buz."

Cohn impatiently spoke aloud. "What I mean to say is that the situation is getting on my nerves. I mean we're alone on this island and can't be said to speak to each other. We may indicate certain things but there's no direct personal communication. I'm not referring to existential loneliness, you understand—what might be called awareness of one's essentially subjective being, not without some sense of death-in-life, if you know what I mean. I'm talking, rather, about the loneliness one feels when he lacks companionship, or that sense of company that derives from community. Do you read me, Buz?"

The chimp signaled, "Drink-fruit (orange or coconut) for Buz."

"First Buz speak to (answer) what I ask (my question)."

The little ape yawned—a gaping pink mouth and lively tongue within a semicircle of strong teeth. His breath smelled like a fragrant mulch pile. Cohn coughed.

Buz attempted to suckle his left nipple.

Cohn dumped him on the ground.

The chimp bit Cohn's right ankle.

He cried out, at once springing a nosebleed. When Buz saw the blood flowing down his upper lip he scampered out of the cave and knuckle-galloped into the forest.

When he was gone two days Cohn worried about him, but on the third day he returned, not without a smirk of guilt, and Cohn forgave him.

Some nights were lonelier than others. They sat by the fire and Buz watched the shadow of Cohn's creaking rocker on the wall. Pointing at it, he let out a gurgling hoot.

"Shadow," Cohn pantomimed, casting a barking dog on the wall with his fingers.

Buz, after studying it, hooted weirdly.

When, as the nights grew warmer, they dispensed with the fire, Cohn, after supper, waited till it was dark, then lit the kerosene lamp if he wanted to read. He read quickly, the kerosene was going fast. When the cave was sultry he read at the table in the hut. There were no moths or mosquitoes invading the lamp. If one could invent a mosquito, Cohn would.

"The silence bugs me."

Buz produced a shrill hoot.

Cohn thanked him.

One night he read to the chimpanzee, regretting he had nothing appropriate for an equivalent of young teenager. But he sensed Buz understood what was read to him; or he understood more than he pretended to. Cohn thought he would try a touch of Shakespeare to attune his ear to spoken English. That might wake a desire to speak the language.

Cohn tried reading aloud from *The Merchant of Venice,* to no avail. Buz was bored and yawned. He studied an illustration on the page and cautiously reached forth a finger to touch Jessica, but Cohn would not let him. Buz retreated, boredom glazing his eyes.

Cohn then switched to Genesis in his Pentateuch and read aloud the story of the first six days of Creation. The chimp listened stilly. On the seventh day, as God rested from His labors, Buz crossed himself. Cohn could not believe he had seen it. Was it a random act? Again he read aloud the Creation, and the ape again crossed himself. Most likely Dr. Bünder had Christianized him, Cohn decided. His thought was that if one of them was a Christian and the other a Jew, Cohn's Island would never be Paradise.

With that in mind he searched in his valise for a black yarmulke he had saved from childhood, then decided not to offer it to Buz. If he wanted to know something about Jewish experience he would have to say so. Jews did not proselytize.

Buz, however, reached for the yarmulke and draped it on his head. That night he slept with it on his forehead, as if he were trying to determine where it would rest most comfortably. He wore it the next day when he made his usual exploratory rounds among the neighboring trees before entering the rain forest, but in the late afternoon he came back without it.

Cohn wanted to know what he had done with it, and got no reply.

He never saw his yarmulke again. Perhaps in some future time, Deo volente, a snake might come slithering along wearing one. Who knows the combinations, transformations, possibilities of a new future?

He offered the chimp the silver crucifix he had been holding for him, but Buz signed for Cohn to retain it since he had no pockets of his own.

Cohn figured that when the chimp hit what might be the equivalent of thirteen years of age, he would offer him a Bar Mitzvah. Buz might accept; he might not. If he didn't, Cohn would give him back his silver cross. I wonder if he thinks he can convert me by letting me hang onto it?

In the meantime he would tell him stories, in particular those he remembered from Aesop, La Fontaine, Dr. Dolittle, and *Tales of the Hasidim*. How else educate someone who couldn't read? Cohn hoped to alter and raise his experiential level—deepen, humanize this sentient, intelligent creature, even though he did not "speak" beyond a variety of hoots and grunts and make a few pantomimed signals.

Besides, Cohn reflected, if I talk to him and he listens, no matter how much or little he comprehends, I hear my own voice and know I am present. And if I am, because I speak to him, maybe one of these days he will reply so that he can be present in my presence. He may get the idea.

Cohn then began a story of his own. "I'm not so good at this," he set it up. "My imagination has little fantasy in it—that's why I became a digger of bones—but I am fairly good at describing what I've seen and lived through. So instead of inventing stories that never happen—although some do anyhow—I'd rather tell you a few items about my past. Let's call it a bit of family history.

"Personally, Buz, I'm the second son of a rabbi who was once a cantor. And he was the first son of a rabbi—my grandfather, alev hasholem—who was killed in a pogrom. That's a word you probably never heard, one

I imagine that Dr. Bünder gave you no sign for."

Buz wouldn't say.

"Nor for Holocaust either? That's a total pogrom and led directly to the Day of Devastation, a tale I will tell you on the next dark day."

The chimp groomed himself under both arms, seeming to be waiting for the real story to commence.

Cohn said that his father the cantor had decided to become a rabbi, and was a good one, thus fulfilling a pledge to his father, not to mention showing respect.

"For somewhat similar reasons I attempted to go the same route, but for complex other reasons I never made it, diverted by inclinations and events I'd rather not talk about at the moment. It isn't that I'm being evasive but there's a time and place for everything."

Cohn, however, mentioned experiencing a trial of faith—losing interest in religion yet maintaining a more than ordinary interest in God Himself.

"It's like staying involved with First Causes but not in their theological consequences. Creation is the mystery that most affects me, so not unexpectedly I ended up in science. And that—to conclude this episode—is why you and I are sitting here listening to each other at a time when nobody else is, I am told."

Cohn, as the chimp yawned, cleverly asked, "And what about yourself? Can you tell me something about you? When and where, for instance, did you meet Dr. Bünder? What influence, in the long run, did he have on you? Are you American by birth, or were you born in Tanzania or Zaire? How did you get on the oceanography vessel, and were you at all aware civilization was ending when the lights banged out and scientists and crew abandoned ship without taking you along? I sense surprising gifts of communication in you and would be grateful, sooner than later, to know the facts."

Buz pointed to his belly button.

"Are you saying you *are*, or asking that question?" Cohn, in rising excitement, wanted to know.

The chimp tried to make his mouth speak. His neck tendons under the decaying cloth bulged as he strained, but no sound came forth—no word, no hoot.

Buz grunted anticlimactically, then leaped up in anger, landing on one foot. He stamped the other, stormed, socked his chest, his body hair rising. There was no crying but he seemed on the verge.

To calm him, Cohn wound up the portable phonograph and put on a record of his father the cantor singing a prayer of lamentation. This was a lamentor indeed; he sang from the pit of his belly, but with respect.

The cantor noisily brayed his passion for

God, pity for the world, compassion for mankind. The force of his fruity baritone seemed to shiver the cave in the rock. His voice was vibrant, youthful; though he was dead. Cohn was grateful his father had died before the Day of Devastation. For that disaster he might not have forgiven God. They had serious trouble after the Holocaust.

"'Sh'ma yisroel, ad-nai eloheynu, ad-nai echad—'" sang the cantor, his wavering voice climbing to the glory of God.

Buz listened in astonishment. He orated, as though complaining. The chimp was holding the lamp above his head, peering at the floor of the cave as if he had encountered a snake. Or discovered a mystery. Was he seeking the source of the cantor's voice? Cohn took the lamp from him and held it to the phonograph. He explained the voice was in the record. The ape, without glancing at it, rushed to the cave opening, pulled aside the vines, and stared into the humid night. Buz's headhair bristled, his canines glowed. He growled in his throat.

"What do you see?" Cohn held the lamp aloft.

The chimp whimpered as a musty hot odor, like a burning tire, or someone's stinkingly sweaty body, with a redemptive trace of mint, flowed into the cave.

Calvin Cohn stared into the primeval night and saw nothing. An essence, unformed and ancient in the night's ripe darkness, caused him to sense he was about to do battle with a dinosaur, if not full-fledged dragon; but he saw neither. Yet he thought he had heard an explosive grunt and had observed a shadow flit out of the hut and into the trees.

Cohn went out in his stocking feet. No stars were visible, but a slender emerald crescent moon was rising. He stood for a while probing the night. When he returned to the cave Buz was snoring as if accompanying a dream of hot pursuit.

In the morning, Cohn returned to his chores in the rice paddy and Buz went exploring. On the way, he played in the acacias and tumbled among the branches of a bushy eucalyptus a little farther down.

He tore off a long leafy branch and leaped to the ground, dragging it up the rocky slope to the escarpment, and then charged down, venting a long scream as he pulled the hissing branch after him. A shower burst on his head as he plunged down the slope. Buz danced like an Indian chief in the rain.

When the rain had let up the next morning, the little chimp went out, stopping to throw rocks at a mangrove tree he didn't like. Before slipping into the rain forest he heaved chunks of coconut shell at two epiphytic trees in the leafy gloom, as if to drive away any lingering evil spirit.

Then he disappeared into the forest, sometimes hooting from trees deep in the green growth. That afternoon when the chimp returned from the rain forest his face seemed gone several shades pale. He covered his shoulders with Cohn's poncho and sat in the chair, hoo-hooting to himself. Cohn squatted, stroking his shoulders, at last quieting him. At dusk he climbed into his acacia sleep-tree and bent some branches back to make a nest for himself, but had second thoughts and slept in the cave.

A quarter moon rose and Buz walked in his sleep. Either that, or he had been frightened as he slept and walked away from the offending sleep-cage.

Cohn asked him if he had had a bad dream but the chimp made no reply.

The next evening, after they had eaten a supper of yams and black beans and drunk tumblers of coconut juice, Cohn played on the phonograph a record of his father the cantor praying. The chimp yodeled along with him, and Cohn, in a sentimental mood, danced to the music of his father's voice. He snapped his thumbs, shook his hips, and sang in Yiddish, "Ich tants far mayn tate."

Buz also tried a few dance steps, dangling one foot, then the other. Abruptly he stopped, his face a frozen sight. What had troubled him? He was these days a nervous chap. Puberty? Cohn wondered. Simply unfulfilled sexual desire? Certainly he was mature enough to want a female—lost cause.

But if there was a female chimp around, Buz wasn't responding in an attractive fashion. Standing at the cave entrance, he pitched into the night a teapot, two tablespoons, a salad bowl Cohn had sculpted with his jackknife and chisel. He had to wrestle two porcelain dishes away from Buz.

Peering through the vines, the chimp bristled and hooted, then retreated, grumbling. Cohn wondered whether the little ape knew something he didn't and ought to?

It seemed to him he heard someone mumbling, or attempting to sing in a guttural voice. It came out a throaty basso aiming an aria to the night sky, possibly pledging his heart and soul to the song of the impassioned cantor. The phonograph was suddenly stilled—silent. Cohn heard nothing more outside the cave. He carried the kerosene lamp to the hut, holding it high so he could see to the edge of the forest.

Amid the shadows wrought in the uneasy night, he had the startled impression he was gazing at a huge man in a black suit seated on the ground twenty feet beyond the hut.

Cohn almost dropped the teetering lamp.

"Who are you?"

The man, rising slowly, became a gorilla lumbering away. When he stopped to look back, his deep, small, black eyes glowed in the lamplight. Cohn wanted frantically to run.

The chimp at the cave stood hooting at the giant ape, preaching against his kind. He shrieked as the gorilla, reversing direction, moved toward him, halting, staring with blank gaze all the more frightening because it seemed to be his only expression.

Cohn ducked into the cave, set down the lamp, and instinctively grabbed a shovel. As though he had touched hot metal, he tossed it aside and reached for an orange.

Buz, sounding more like monkey than ape, retreated as the gorilla loomed up at the cave entrance. A musty, rank, yet heavy herbal odor filled the cave.

Cohn in a quick whisper warned Buz to quiet down, but the half-hysterical animal, scooping a coconut off the shelf, pitched it at the gorilla. It bounced with a thud off his sloping skull, yet his eyes did not flicker in the lamplight as he stared at the two frightened inhabitants of the cave.

Cohn, sotto voce, informed Buz that the gorilla would not attack if he did not bother him. "But he will rend you limb from limb if you act like a hysteric."

The chimp protested this strategy, but the gorilla, as if he had decided he would never make a home in this cave, mercifully fell back, turning again to cast an impassive stare at them. Or was it a depressive type they were contending with? As he knuckle-walked to the rain forest he expelled a burst of gorilla gas and was gone.

Cohn wondered how many more apes, large or small, he must confront if the Lord's computer had stopped telling Him the numerical truth.

* * *

The next morning the gorilla sat alone under a bearded palm tree fifty feet from the cave.

He seems a peaceful gent, Cohn thought, and I'll pretend he isn't there unless he gives me a sign to the contrary.

He was a burly beast, almost ugly, with a shaggy blue-black head and heavy brow ridges. His nostrils were highlighted like polished black stones, and his mouth, when he yawned, was cavernous. The gorilla's black coat was graying on his massive shoulders. Still, if he was frightening, he was not frightful. Despite his size and implied strength—perhaps because he seemed to have a talented ear for devotional music—there was something gentle about him. His dark brown eyes seemed experienced, saddened—after the Flood?—in a way Buz's weren't. Cohn respected the giant ape.

All morning he had remained nearby, as though listening, waiting perhaps to hear the cantor singing. No doubt he was looking for company. Cohn asked Buz not to disturb him. A large friend in a small world had its advantages. But Buz, though he listened obediently, at least respectfully, on catching sight of the gorilla sitting under his favorite white acacia, persistently banged an aluminum frying pan against the escarpment until it howled like a metal drum. He orated at length, growing hoarse, and barking like a baboon. But the gorilla sat motionlessly watching.

Cohn figured he might put on a phonograph record to test his theory; instead he ventured forth and sat in the grass about ten feet from the gorilla, his heart pounding. One false move—for instance, threatening the beast by staring into his eyes—and goodbye Cohn.

Calvin Cohn then experienced an extraordinary insight: I know this one. I know his scent. We've met before.

"Are you the one," he asked humbly, "who fed me when I was sick? If so, please accept heartfelt thanks."

The gorilla blinked as though he wasn't sure he understood the question. He stared at Cohn as if he might have helped him, or he might not; he had his mystery.

Cohn cautiously approached the huge animal—he weighed a good five hundred pounds—with extended hand, his gaze on the ground.

The gorilla rose on his short legs, as he watched the man coming toward him, and modestly raised his own right arm. But Buz, spying the gesture, ran between them, screeching, before the extended arms could become a handclasp.

Although Cohn tried to restrain the jealous chimp, Buz chattered at the gorilla, taunting him.

The chimp pretend-charged, backed off, lunged forward as if to attack, but the gorilla patiently fended him off with his meaty long arm. Grunting at the chimp, he knuckle-walked away. He lifted himself into an acacia tree and sat on a low bough in the dappled sunlight, peacefully observing the scene below.

A true gentleman, Cohn thought.

"If it's all right with you," he addressed the gorilla in gratitude, "I'd like to call you George, after my late wife's father, who was an accomplished dentist, a wonderful man. He often fixed people's teeth for nothing."

He told the gorilla they three were alone in the world and must look after each other.

George seemed to agree, but Buz had clapped both hands over his ears and was mockingly hooting.

One early morning Cohn, on awaking, stealthily drew aside the vines and let in the light. Since Buz was asleep in his cage, he tiptoed over with a pair of small scissors, and reaching between the wooden bars before the ape was thoroughly awake, snipped off his fetid, decomposing neck cloth.

The wound he expected to see was totally healed, and from it two flattened copper wires grew out of the scar where a man's Adam's apple would be.

Buz, awaking startled, hoarsely protested

the loss of his loving compress, but Cohn argued it needed a washing and dropped it into the dirty-laundry basket. Buz then did his business outside the cave, as he had been taught; and when he returned, Cohn, before serving him his banana-rice porridge, got the chimp to play tickle.

As he tickled Buz under the arms, he lifted the hilarious ape into a chair, and deftly twisted together the two exposed copper wires on his neck. There was a momentary crackling as the chimp, grinning sickly, stared at Cohn, and Cohn, smiling sheepishly, observed him. After a rasping cough, followed by a metallic gasp that startled him, Buz spoke as though reciting a miracle.

"Fontostisch/// I con hear myzelv speag/// pong-pong."

Hearing his words, Buz in joy jumped off and on his chair in celebration. Displaying proudly, he socked his chest with both fists. The chimp, then emitting a piercing hoot, rushed out of the cave, shinnied up a nearby palm tree, tore off a fan-shaped leafy branch, and charged up the rocky slope, dragging the swishing branch behind him.

"Fontostisch///" he exclaimed as he knuckle-galloped down the slope with his palm branch. "I con talg/// pong-pong."

Calvin Cohn, flushed with the excitement of unexpected adventure, could almost not believe what he had heard.

"A miracle," he conceded. "But what do you mean by pong-pong?"

"Thot's nod me/// Thot's the sound the copper wires mage when they vibrate ot the end of a sendence/// I hov on artifiziol lorynch/// pong-pong."

His voice was metallic, as if he were a deaf person talking, who had never before heard himself articulate. Buz spoke with his juicy tongue awash in his mouth. His speech, reminiscent of Dr. Bünder's, sounded like a metachimp's, given that possibility. In any case, that the ape could speak had fired Cohn's imagination.

"How do you know what a sentence is?"

"I con understond and speag only words I hov formerly heard/// pong-pong. I con say whot I hov heard you say to me/// I con alzo say those words thot Dr. Bünder taught me/// For instonze, I know the Lord's Prayer/// pong-pong."

"How did he teach you that?"

"He taught it to me in sign longuoge/// but now I know it is words thot I hov in my head/// pong-pong."

"Did he perform the operation on your larynx?"

Buz coughed metallically. "If he hod waited another weeg or two I would hov done it myzelf/// I was already talging on my libs but he didn't hear it/// I would hov talged oz I do now/// pong-pong."

"How—without a proper larynx?"

"Because onimals con talg///" Buz told him. "We talg among ourselves/// Maybe someday you will hear our phonemes oz we hear yours/// If you con communicade with one living onimal/// you con communicade with all his relations/// It is pozzible if you will odmid the pozzibility///"

Cohn said it seemed a reasonable possibility. "Belief itself may not be that easy, but I want to believe. In fact, after hearing you in action, I do. I imagine your experience contains an evolutionary factor in it, and I see it as real and believable."

Cohn went on: "What an extraordinary opportunity it provides to understand the nature of communication and development of speech in man. I bet I could make an important contribution in semantics, and I greatly regret there's no one but us, and maybe George, to behold this miracle."

"There's Jesus of Nozoroth///" Buz said.

"Maybe," said Cohn.

Buz said that was beyond question.

Withal a miracle, Cohn felt; he was deeply moved, still amazed, all but overwhelmed. Despite his eccentricities Dr. Walther Bünder had been an extraordinary scientist; and Buz—God bless—was a genius chimp.

Now I will have an intelligent companion as long as we both shall live. Cohn dabbed his eyes with his woolen handkerchief.

The chimp, observing this, tried to squeeze out a tear but failed.

Cohn said not to worry, he would teach him how, among other things.

"Sholl I call you moster/// pong-pong?"

"Call me Cal, or if you like, call me Dad."

"Dod///" said Buz, "pong-pong."

Cohn, with a pair of ratnose pliers, tightened Buz's neck wires, and that ended the pong-pong. The chimp said he hadn't minded the redundant sound so long as he could clearly say the rest of a sentence. His articulation improved, and in a short while he lost almost every trace of Dr. Bünder's accent and enunciated consonants and most vowels correctly.

Cohn praised him for being a good lad. They laid arms around each other and affectionately kissed.

Buz began his language studies diligently assisted by Cohn, who read him selected pages in the dictionary. Cohn redefined the definitions, not always to Buz's satisfaction. At first the chimp felt a word should mean what it looked like. He wanted an aardvark to be a snail in its shell, hoping the aard was the snail and the vark its cubicle. Later he accepted the aardvark as a termite eater and called the snail a disgusting slug.

Their dictionary study pleased Buz, and he wondered if it would improve his vocabulary if he ate a few pages now and then, but Cohn forbade that for all time.

Nonetheless he made satisfactory progress. He was not timid in guessing the meaning of words he didn't know, that Cohn used, and asking about others. One day he had a remarkable insight: "What you don't say means something too." Cohn agreed. That was a breakthrough point, and thereafter Buz made faster progress in his mastery of language. Cohn was overjoyed by his semantic talent.

Buz one day wanted to know who had invented language.

Cohn said man. "That's what made him superior to all the other creatures."

"If he was so superior where is he now?"

"Here I am," said Cohn.

"I mean the humon race?"

Cohn, on reflection, admitted maybe God had invented language. "The word began the world. Nor would anyone have known there was a monotheistic God if He hadn't proclaimed it."

Buz said that maybe Jesus had invented language.

Cohn said, "He spoke well but the word was already there."

"He preached to the chimps," said Buz.

Cohn said that Buz had just got close to a metaphor and praised him.

"How close?"

"The chimps as Christians."

"Whot's a metaphor?"

"It's a symbol—sort of," Cohn responded.

"It says something not fully expected, through analogy. Like when a banana is conceived to symbolize a man's phallus, and a cave or grotto, a womb."

"I don't agree that a cave is a wombot," Buz said.

"Womb, not wombat."

"I don't believe it. I don't think a phollus is a bonona. I eat bononas, I don't eat phol-luses."

"Eating has nothing to do with it. An object, because of a quality in common with another, is taken to represent the other. For instance, Walt Whitman in one of his poems refers to the grass as 'the handkerchief of the Lord'—far out but reasonable."

Buz said he wished his name was Walt.

"Your name is Buz."

"I wish it was Walt. Why does he call the grass a handkerchief?"

"It provides an earthly concept of God: He who walks on grass with the same ease as he uses His handkerchief. Or He may use the grass to wipe His brow. Anyway, He dwells in our lives. Another similar concept is God the Father."

"Whot about God the son?"

"That's a metaphor too."

Buz said it was the one he liked the best.

"You take your choice," Cohn said. "In any case, it's through language that a man becomes more finely and subtly man—a sensitive, principled, civilized human being—as he opens himself to other men—by comprehending, describing, and communicating his experiences, aspirations, and nature—such as it is. Or was." Cohn smiled a melancholy smile.

"Don't forget the chimponzees," Buz said.

He afterwards asked, "If I go on learning your longuoge will I become humon?"

"Maybe not you yourself," Cohn replied, "but something like that could happen in the long run." He said his descent and Buz's from a common ancestor had been a matter of eons of evolution. "And if it was to happen again, I hope it results in an improved species of homo sapiens."

"Whot is humon, Dod?"

Cohn said he thought to be human was to be responsive to and protective of life and civilization.

Buz said he would rather be a chimp.

He wanted to know where stories came from.

Cohn said from other stories.

"Where did they come from?"

"Somebody spoke a metaphor and that broke into a story. Man began to tell them to keep his life from washing away."

"Which was the first story?"

"God inventing Himself."

"How did He do thot?"

"He began, He's the God of Beginnings. He

said the word and the earth began. If you tell stories you can say what God's doing. Let's read that one again, Buz." He turned to the story of Creation.

Buz said he was tired of that one. "Nothing hoppons in thot fairy story. Why don't you read about Jesus of Nozoroth? He preached to the chimponzees."

"In what language?"

"I don't know thot. We heard His voice in our ears."

Cohn said he didn't have a copy of the New Testament in the cave. He did have the Old.

"Tell it without the book."

He would, promised Cohn. "But you complain I don't tell you enough animal stories, so how about one of those now? I'll start with the old snake who lived in Paradise with Adam and Eve."

Buz said he hated snake stories. "They crawl on their bellies."

Cohn said God had punished them for getting man into trouble. "Rashi—he was a medieval Talmudic commentator—in other words, somebody who told stories about stories—he said the snake saw Adam and Eve having intercourse amid the flowers. The snake afterwards asked Eve for a bit of the same, but she indignantly refused. That started off his evil plans of the betrayal of man. I've read you the story where he tempted Eve with the apple. She could have said no, but the snake was a tricky gent. He got her confused by his sexual request."

"Whot's intercourse?"

"I read you the relevant passage in Dr. Bünder's book."

"When will I get some of it?"

Cohn said he was sorry but couldn't say.

"If not the snake, how about Cain and Abel?" he asked. "There's action in that one, a stupendous blow on the head."

Buz said he disliked violence and bloodshed. He said he preferred the New Testament.

"There's plenty of violence and blood in the New Testament. Painters worked in red from that for centuries."

"Thot's because they crucified Jesus of Nozoroth," Buz said.

"Who did?" asked Cohn, on the qui vive.

"The Roman soldiers."

Cohn patted his head.

"Tell me the one about the Dod who cut his little boy's throat," Buz then asked.

Cohn responded in annoyance. "Buz, I've told you four times that Abraham never cut his boy's throat. Those who said he did were making up stories that suited their own natures, not Isaac's or Abraham's."

"Tell me again," sighed Buz, climbing up on Calvin Cohn's lap.

Cohn told him again: "This is the story of

Abraham and Isaac, his beloved son," he began. "The Talmud says that Satan pestered God to test Abraham's love for Him; and God, to test and prove that love, commanded Abraham to take his boy up to the mountain in Moriah and give him for a burnt offering to the Lord Himself.

"As the story goes, Abraham, not flicking an eyelash, out of love for God, consented. Isaac carried the wood for the fire up the mountain. Then Abraham laid it on the altar, binding his son with leather thongs before lifting the knife to his throat."

Buz said the story was giving him cramps.

"Then why do you ask me to tell it?"

Buz thought maybe it was the figs he had eaten for breakfast that gave him cramps. "But tell the story anyway."

Cohn went on: "Just as Abraham was about to sacrifice his son, an angel called to him out of the blue, 'Don't lay your hands on that boy, or do anything to hurt him. I know you fear God.' And that proves that the Lord, at any given time, may not know all, or He would surely have known that Abraham feared Him.

"On the other hand, if God was testing Abraham to get Satan off His back, He knew what the outcome would be, and I bet Satan did—he has his talents—but not Abraham or Isaac. Still and all, their suffering was limited more or less to intense worry, and had no discernible traumatic effect after the incident when they had confirmed the hard way that they all loved each other."

Buz liked happy endings. "God is love," he said.

Cohn wasn't sure but didn't say so.

"So Isaac's life was saved," he quickly went on, "and a ram caught by his horns in a thicket was substituted as the burnt offering, in that way affirming the idea of an animal in place of human sacrifice. I'm talking now about the time the story of Abraham and Isaac began to be told. It was probably a protest against the pagan sacrifice of human beings. That's what I meant by man humanizing himself—if you follow me."

"Ond do you call murdering onimols a civilized oct?" Buz wanted to know.

Before Cohn, embarrassed, could reply, a rumble of thunder shook the sandstone escarpment. Dirt and small stones sifted down from the ceiling. Fearing an earthquake, or worse, Cohn, cowering over Buz, listened for God's judgment but heard none. He had broken into a chilling sweat and warned himself to be very careful what he was saying. Apparently God wasn't liking every word of it.

"Whot hopponed?" Buz asked, hauling himself out from under Cohn.

"Thunder and lightning."

"Is thot bod?"

"It depends on His mood."

Cohn hesitantly returned to the story of Isaac, saying: "That ended his ordeal, except that if you reflect on the details at the very end, you figure he must have got lost on the mountain after his life was saved by the Angel, because he disappears from the tale. Exit Isaac. The scriptures have them both going up the mountain to participate in the ceremony God had ordained, but only Abraham came down. So where was Isaac?"

Buz, clearly in suspense, said he had no idea.

Cohn said some Talmudic sages had interpreted it that Isaac had been carried off by the Angel to the Garden of Eden, and that he had rested there, convalescing from the bloody wound his father had inflicted on him.

"Thot's whot I said, but you got mod ot me."

Cohn replied the true reading obviously was that Abraham had not cut his son's throat—God wouldn't allow it—no matter what Abraham's intention, conscious or otherwise, may have been.

"A certain philosopher—somebody called Kierkegaard, whom I haven't told you about, though he's on my list to bring up—he felt that Abraham really wanted to murder Isaac. Freud might have agreed—I'll be filling you in on him in the very near future."

"Do I hov to know everything?" Buz complained. He hopped off Cohn's lap, circled the cave, then climbed back on him.

Cohn loved explication—had once considered becoming a teacher. "Everything that counts," he replied. "Which leads to why the interpretation of Abraham as his son's cutthroat persists through the centuries. That says something about the nature of man—his fantasies of death that get enacted into the slaughter of man by man—kinfolk or strangers in droves—on every possible mindless occasion. But let's not go into that now, except to point out that man paid for who he was—maybe—to my mind—er—somewhat unjustly."

He glanced uneasily at the split up in the ceiling, yet still ran on. "When you bring it all back to basics," he whispered, "it means that God made man seriously imperfect. Maybe what was on His mind was that if He made man whole, pacific, good, he would feel no need to become better, and if he didn't, he would never truly be a man. He also planned it that man had to contend with evil, or it was no go. But the awful thing was that the evil was much a bigger bag of snakes than man could handle. We behaved toward each other like animals, and therefore the Second Flood followed hard on the Day of Devastation."

Buz hooted, "I'm on onimol and hov always been a vegetorion."

Cohn complimented him and hastily returned to Isaac lost on the mountain. "How do you think he got down?"

Buz suggested that maybe a kidnapper had kidnapped him.

Cohn said that might have happened. "But murdered, kidnapped, or whatever, he got to Paradise—some commentators said. There he was resurrected, they say. That's a twist in the story that shows the human passion to bring the dead back to life. Given the nature of death—how long it lasts once it sets in—who can blame us for inventing resurrection?"

Cohn said his personal opinion was that man's will to hang on to life was a worthy reason why God should have preserved humanity. "Call it upholding the value of His original investment."

"Jesus of Nozoroth was resurrected," Buz said.

Cohn said that resurrection was probably related to the resurrection of Isaac. "The New Testament scribes always set the Christian unfolding carefully in the Judaic past."

"Jesus was the first," Buz said. "He preached to the chimps."

Cohn said that whoever was first, neither Judaism nor Christianity, nor any other religion, had prevented the Day of Devastation.

"Well, that's the end of that story," he told Buz, "except that the Talmudists say Isaac returned from Paradise after three years, to his father's house, and soon began to look for a bride. According to the commentators, he was thirty-seven years old when the incident of the burnt offering occurred—and even given the evidence, that's an astonishment."

The chimp, after sitting a moment in silence, asked, "When will I get morried, Dod?"

Cohn, genuinely moved, said he didn't see how that could happen just then. "I'm afraid there's nobody on this island you can marry."

"Con't I morry you?"

Cohn, though he appreciated the sentiment, said it wouldn't work. But he admitted, "We are sort of married in the sense that we are living together and sharing a similar fate."

Buz was disappointed.

Cohn said he hoped Buz had anyway enjoyed his retelling of the story of Abraham and Isaac, though it seemed to get more involved every time he retold it.

Buz said he thought it was a pretty simple story.

During the season of rains, confined to the cave for days, they were often bored. Cohn continued to relate stories of his father—peace on his head. When the old Cohn was seventy-five, he cut into his long white beard to have a better look at his lifelong face. The chimp got a pair of scissors out of the toolbox and began to snip at his own skimpy beard, but Cohn took them away.

On wet days Cohn would sometimes dim the kerosene lamp and, in the shadowy cave, as it windily poured outside, would play records on the wind-up portable phonograph.

Despite the force of the gale, George the gorilla sat under a dripping acacia, soaked to the skin, his drenched head bent to his chest as he listened through the wind to the vibrant bray of Cohn's father the cantor.

But when the gorilla, as the downpour lightened, or momentarily ceased, attempted to edge closer to the cave, Buz, who often peeked through the curtain of vines to follow George's movements when he was in the vicinity, flung stones, spoons, bamboo sticks at him. And when he ran out of ammunition, he threw cups and saucers and carved wooden figurines, despite Cohn's ringing disapproval.

Cohn, when the rain let up long enough for him to venture forth in his orange oilskins, occasionally came upon George as they were seeking tubers, or fruit, in the woodland. One day as they stood a short distance apart, Cohn tried to express his apologies to George for the chimp's immature behavior. He said he hoped Buz would soon get used to George; he was a little on the fearful side—despite his intelligence—having been traumatized as a child by being separated from his mother by a scientist who had cut into his neck for reasons of experiment. George raised his hand to touch his throat, then turned and plunged off. That was as much direct communication as they had experienced up to then, but Cohn was not disheartened.

Having George nearby, however, had certain disadvantages. The gorilla, who lived on grasses, roots, bark, bamboo pith, also seemed to relish fruit for dessert, and some of the fruit trees, when he was in residence, were all but denuded after George had been out collecting. He was a connoisseur and would fling aside fifty bitter mangoes to find one sweet one. Cohn couldn't stand the waste.

Yet he felt sorry for the animal—gorillas were polygamous family types, and George had no one to go home to. He was a wanderer in the forest and wandered alone; Cohn could hear him swishing through the vegetation. He often thought, when they passed each other in a clearing, of asking him to the cave for an occasional meal, but when he tried in sign language—pointing to his mouth with his finger—to convey an invitation that George return with him for a fruit-salad dessert plus a cup of banana beer, the wary great ape, his dark brown eyes lonelily observing Cohn, made mournful growling noises.

Cohn had more than once attempted to follow George in the forest, but the gorilla screamed and trumpeted his displeasure, and Cohn hastened away. One day he decided to hold his ground when he encountered the great ape, and for an uneasy moment he watched George approach bipedally. Cohn, as advised in Dr. Bünder's book, lowered his eyes and stared at his toes as George came forward and noisily sniffed Cohn's head and ears, then slunk away as if affronted by the odor.

But he was back as though by appointment, rain or shine, when the cantor was singing in the phonograph. The chimp, after an initial lively response to the old man praying, now stuffed his fingers into his ears and orated against the noise. George, on the other hand, listening outside the cave, after a magnificent Kaddish, rose to his full height and pounded his chest as if it were a kettledrum.

When the chimp heard the gorilla booming his breast he hid in the rear of the cave and covered his head with dirty laundry.

George also liked to be present when Cohn, preferably in the hut, but also in the cave, from which his voice could be heard, was reading aloud to Buz or telling him stories. The gorilla listened as though he understood every word—though sometimes his eyes expressed puzzlement—of Cohn's tales, particularly those about his father the rabbi. George would grunt, perhaps was affected by an act of mercy the old man had engaged in, as when he had labored up the stairs of a cold tenement to deliver a pail of coal to an old woman in a freezing flat.

And Cohn could hear the gorilla breathing in suspense as he read aloud, for instance, of the escape of the Israelites across the parted Red Sea, pursued furiously by hordes of Egyptian charioteers. When the waves of the sea crashed on their heads, and horses and men drowned embracing, George cried out as though in woe. Cohn felt that the gorilla was on the verge of speech even if he hadn't yet learned sign language. There was no saying what the future might bring. Cohn hoped someday to ask George how he had been saved from the Devastation. Had God appeared to him, and if He had, in what language had they conversed?

As the windy, lashing rains diminished, the soaked earth gave forth miniature gold orchids, lilies, poinsettias. And mimosas, acacias, jacarandas burst into yellow, red, purple blossoms. After the rain they listened to water dripping from leaf to leaf in the trees. The chimp sat on Cohn's lap after a sit-wrestle, which was work. Buz was a big lad now, growing taller, stronger. Cohn had begun to build him a rocker of his own to sit in as he listened to stories.

Now Cohn was quietly talking about the gorilla to his boy. He asked Buz to be nice to him. "He's gentle and does no harm to anybody. He hangs around this cave because he's lonely. He's a family type, it says in the ape book."

"He looks mean to me," Buz said. "If he ever cotches me in the forest on a dark night, he will eat me up."

"He wouldn't eat a cockroach. Gorillas are herbivores."

"I don't like his name either."

"What would you have suggested?" Cohn had stiffened a little.

"Adolph."

"Over my dead body." Cohn said he had named the gorilla after a fine dentist he knew, but also after George Washington; and he told Buz the story of the cherry tree. He warned the chimp that the more sticks and stones he flung at George, the more Buz's fear of him would grow.

"Try a little love," Cohn suggested.

"I don't see what love hos to do with thot fot gorilla. You said thot if it didn't work before the Flood why should it work ofter?"

"These are different times," Cohn explained. "As we progress, what didn't work in the past may work hereafter."

"I know thot," Buz answered, "but does thot stupid gorilla?"

Someone close by coughed, and they discovered George outside, sitting against the wall of the escarpment. Seeing himself discovered, the embarrassed gorilla rose and knuckle-lumbered away.

The chimp, hopping on both legs, cried murder. "He's a fot, stupid pig, and besides thot, he stinks."

Cohn warned him not to start that kind of talk. "How often must I tell you of the Devastation that destroyed the world and every living being except you, me, and George? If we expect to go on living we have to be kind to each other."

The chimp, in disgust, climbed the wall shelves and sat on the top, as far from Cohn as he could. He spent most of the day in his hammock outside the cave.

On his return from the rice paddies the next afternoon, Cohn hunted for a record whose melody he had been humming that morning.

He found the carton of records where he kept them, high on the wooden shelves, but couldn't locate the one he wanted. Counting them, Cohn, to his dismay, found that one was missing—there were nine instead of ten.

Had Buz taken it to punish his dod for something? Disturbed, Cohn rushed out of the cave looking for the chimp. Instead of Buz he spied George the gorilla seated in a eucalyptus, in mid-tree, steadying himself by holding onto an overhead branch, as he chewed on the phonograph record he held in his hand. He had taken a large bite and was trying to savor it as he crackingly chewed. Then George spat it out and flung the record away. It sailed in the air like a frisbee and struck the escarpment, breaking into bits.

Cohn uttered a brokenhearted sob. "Bastard-fool," he shouted, "I'll shoot you dead if you ever again enter the cave without my permission."

George hastily lowered himself to the bottom limb and dropped to the ground. He ran into the rain forest like a runaway locomotive.

During the spring they explored the far end of the island, after beaching the rubber raft near a stunted palm.

"Tie it up," Cohn ordered. "There's nothing in sight, but one never knows."

He was wearing his poncho and rain-repellent fur hat after a chest cold two weeks before. His voice was hoarse. Cohn carried a 30.06 Winchester 70 rifle he had discovered on the last trip to the *Rebekah Q*. Why he had brought it along on his present jaunt into the far country, he wasn't sure. He had over oiled the weapon, and the dripping barrel smelled.

It was a large gun and Cohn was uneasy about leaving it behind just anywhere, as they were exploring. A stupid fear, really atavistic. It should have gone out with the Devastation, but somehow persisted.

Buz wore a Venetian gondolier's red-ribboned straw hat he had found in Dr. Bünder's clothes closet, and was otherwise unclothed. He had recently tried on a pair of Cohn's winter drawers but they did not fit well. In fact, he had burst through two pairs before giving up.

He carried along an aluminum oar, at times resting it on his shoulder in the same military fashion Cohn held the Winchester. As they were exploring a low sandstone outcropping about two miles from shore, Cohn stopped, speechless, his throat constricted, and pointed to a blob of semi-liquid dark matter he had almost stepped into.

Buz raised his oar to kill the creature, but Cohn, gone fearfully pale, grabbed the ape's arm, hoarsely crying, "Don't, it will splatter us. It's an animal spoor."

"Whot's thot?"

"In this case, animal droppings—excrement."

"Shit?"

"More or less, though I don't care for that word on this island."

"It's the gorilla!"

Cohn didn't think so. "A gorilla's dung tends to be a dry, fibrous, three-lobed dropping. This is semi-liquid without signs of fiber."

"I say it's thot stupid gorilla. It smells like him."

"What would he be doing up here in the headlands?"

"He's spying on us."

"What in the world for?"

"Because he's a spy and thot's whot they do. He follows us and hears whot we say."

"Whatever animal this derived from," Cohn said uneasily, "I don't want to think about. Let's get out of here and head back to the cave."

"Suppose it's a lady?"

Cohn, on reexamining the turd, said he hadn't thought of that.

When they returned to the stunted palm at the beach where they had moored the raft, to their dismay and stupefaction it was gone. Cohn, shading his eyes, saw a yellow speck on the distant water, floating away. Buz lamented he had left a bag of dried figs in it.

"I was depending on that raft to get us off this island someday," Cohn muttered. "There has to be another island, maybe a piece of what was once African coast floating around. Given the few tools we have, it will take us months to construct a usable boat."

He turned in annoyance to Buz. "How did it happen? I told you to tie the raft to the palm tree."

Buz confessed he hadn't learned to tie a decent knot. "My fingers don't know how to make one."

"Why in Christ's name didn't you tell me?"

"I didn't wont you to swear ot me."

Cohn denied it in exasperation. "Have I ever sworn at you?"

"I heard you curse thot gorilla."

"There's a difference between curse and curse out," Cohn explained, but the chimp seemed doubtful.

They shouldered arms and began the long trek across the island to their cave.

From time to time Cohn stopped to shoot a rifle bullet in practice. Whenever he fell on his knee to fire, Buz ran for shelter.

* * *

The night they arrived at the cave, Buz sat on Cohn's lap and asked for a story.

Cohn told him he thought that the story one heard most probably became the one he would live out.

Buz then said he didn't want to hear one.

But Cohn, in a mood for talk, told Buz that a philosopher by the name of Ortega y Gasset once said that the difference between a man and a chimp is that the chimp wakes every morning as if no other chimpanzee had existed before him.

Buz didn't like that philosopher. "I think of my mother, and I think of Dr. Bünder."

"He was no chimp," Cohn said.

Buz said he could have been one.

Cohn said he was curious about how Buz had managed to escape death on the Day of Devastation.

"I hid in the toilet."

"Why didn't Dr. Bünder take you with him?"

The chimp's voice wavered. "He said in my ear thot he didn't wont me to drown in the ocean."

"So he left you on the ship and took to a lifeboat?"

Buz reminded Cohn that he was the one who was alive and not Dr. Bünder. "But I am grateful for whot he did for me." He said he thought they ought to change the name of the island to Dr. Walther Bünder Island, but Cohn did not favor the idea.

He said he would rather call it Survivor's Island. "Survive is what we have to do. Thus we protest our fate to God and at the same time imitate Him."

"Whot for?"

"My father said survival was one way we shared God's purpose."

Buz, vaguely fingering his pink phallus, said his opinion was that the true purpose of life was to have as much fun as one could.

Cohn separated his hand from his organ. "Leave it alone, let it breathe."

Buz bristled, hair thickening.

"Leave it alone," Cohn insisted, "until you know what to do with it, sexually speaking."

"Why don't you tell me, instead of twisting my arm?"

Cohn apologized. "Sex ties up with survival," he explained, "not to speak of certain pleasures of creation. For survival the participants need someone of the opposite sex and neither of us is that. Given the nature of things, that limits possibility."

Buz stealthily tried to slip his fingers between Cohn's thighs, and though his dod knew it was meant benignly he would not allow his boy to touch his testicles.

Buz snuggled close and was soon sucking Cohn's nipple through Dr. Bünder's white silk shirt. The tug of the chimp's insistent lips on his dry nipple hurt, but Cohn let him suck.

Outside the cave, George, peeking through the ivy curtain, stared at the sight, but when Cohn looked up he let go of the ivy and scampered off.

Jealous? Shocked? Outraged? Cohn wondered. He gazed down at the little chimp at his breast.

If you had suckled the lad, could you marry him?

The Schooltree

God was silent.

Cohn tried to squeeze out a small assurance. That had its dangers: Would He respond to preserve me, or would that remind Him to knock me off?

Why would He do that? Cohn thought. I'm the only man left—no serious threat to Him. Why don't I simply give notice I'm still around, and hope it helps because He enjoys the attention I give Him?

On the other hand, I could forget the whole business and pray He forgets me.

(I could also ask, if He responds, "Why does God permit evil?"

""How could I not?""

Touché.)

Cohn tried prayer to establish contact but no vibrations occurred, and in muddled desperation he flung a coconut at the night sky.

The fruit ascended and never descended, not as fruit. Something happened on high—perhaps the coconut struck an astral body or itself became one?

Whatever caused what, Cohn couldn't say, but a contained cosmic bang occurred from whose center a flaring stream of flame shot forth. Watching in wonder, Cohn concluded this was no meteor in flight, but a twisting hard fire with his initials on it—for Curse Cohn? Clobber or Castrate Cohn?

He hurried to his protective cave, and though a long day passed as he lay hidden under a rock ledge, Cohn heard no punitive spat of electric, no hiss of flame, boom of thunder, or driving rain. The hidden man imagined the coconut had whizzed past God's good ear, Who wrote in icy letters in the sky, ""Don't make waves!"" Then more gently, ""Don't call anything to my attention; I will call it to yours.""

Cohn remembered: God was Torah. He was made of words.

Cohn suggested a census to Buz, "Of every bug, to see if any are present."

Though they roamed the breadth of the island, poking into mounds, webs, combs, and dry holes, they located no ants, spiders, roaches—no flies or bedbugs either.

The Lord had wiped the island clean of insects—no buzzing except Buz, who groomed himself under both arms and discovered no single louse or flea.

Meandering homeward, they explored a moist deep cave one would think might harbor a waterbug or two; but it contained no more than a network of labyrinthine galleries, narrow and broad, which led crookedly to others where stalactites hung like icicles from stone ceilings, dripping glowing drops on the limestone stumps rising from sweating floors.

After a long descent through shadowy corridors lit by Cohn's white candle stub in his wax-stippled hand, they discovered that this mountainful of twisting chambers at last opened on a sparkling sand beach by the restless, booming sea.

Buz hopped with joy at the sight, and Cohn fell to his knees in the white sand, ravished by the view of purple waves breaking and spilling over a line of black rocks along the shore, and flowing as lit foam up the beach.

They swam in the refreshing water and afterwards ascended the mountain into a long cave crowded with crystalline columns. The walls gave forth mysterious noises, as though of voices whispering, or muted singing in the rocks; but no living creatures, not even a small fish, dwelt anywhere they could see or hear.

* * *

"I say a hundred," Buz swore, panting like an exhausted messenger.

Cohn, cleaning a fossilized spinal column of a small ancient horse, possibly Eohippus, that he had dug up in a rocky field beyond the rice paddy, suggested maybe a dozen?

"Droves," Buz swore, swaggering from foot to foot.

"Would you say ten?"

The ape jumped two feet in annoyance, hitting the ground on his fours.

Cohn, abandoning skepticism, cast aside his leather apron and hurried after Buz into the trees below the cave. These were separated by a grassy sward from the edge of the rain forest.

There in the woodland, halfway up a massive, scarred baobab that looked like a ruined tree crossed with an abandoned tenement house of a former world, appeared—great heavens!—five unknown chimpanzees huddled together on a bough whose girth was that of an ordinary tree trunk. The five apes had been exploring the baobab, but when Cohn approached, a warning hoot drove them together.

The tree, whose top looked like an arthritic human hand, seemed to have been stripped of its fruit, leaves, yards of bark, by the famished, hyperactive, shabby apes, who looked as if they had been recently released from a prison pit, and had spent their first hours of freedom devouring the baobab. Their bellies had popped out—but their faces were gaunt. On the ground around its trunk lay piles of hard-shelled green fruits spilling their mucilaginous pulp.

Calvin Cohn stared at the strangers in the tree, momentarily stunned. He found the sight, real as it was, difficult to believe. If there was no single live insect on the island, where did five living chimps come from?

Studying them, Cohn discovered a young female holding a pendulous white flower; and a graybeard male with rheumy eyes and a chest cold; also a gorilla-like, sour-faced, youthful male, who bristled at Cohn—and two squinting skinny male children, apparently younger than Buz, with relatively large heads, low-lying eyes, and short extremities. Both peered stilly at Cohn as he observed them. They were surely twins. He could hear them rhythmically breathing.

"Where are you from?" Cohn asked, and the five startled apes, as if they had been whistled to, broke their huddle and disappeared into the forest.

Cohn, considering hot pursuit, paused to reflect. He must find out where they had come from and how escaped Devastation and Flood. Suppose—as the five chimps unexpectedly were—another human being, possibly female, was also alive on the island? Though Cohn believed that only he, of all men, had been more or less spared—who, on this further evidence of the Lord's occasional inattentiveness to events on earth, could be certain?

If he pursued, they would easily outdistance him. Better he woo them with bananas. Cohn hurried to the cave for a ripe basketful—this was the best red-banana season ever—and then hastened into the forest, trailing Buz. The little ape, having watched Cohn's encounter with the newly arrived chimps, from a discreet distance, now swung on lianas from tree to tree, as his dod, carrying the banana basket, plowed through the vegetation below, depending on Buz to alert him when he sighted the apes.

Within minutes they came upon the newcomers, now dispersed on five limbs of an ebony tree. They were a genuinely tired lot, the female an attractive but wilted creature, the males grubby, their unkempt coats missing patches of hair, their eyes listless, still showing hunger. Only the barrel-chested male seemed energetic. Seeing Cohn, he rose threateningly, but was immediately affected by the banana basket, at whose contents he stared greedily.

Cohn set the basket down under the ebony tree and though the two boys came to life, whimpering in anticipation, none of the apes descended the tree to get at the bananas.

"Eat if you please," Cohn announced, and nobody moved.

Buz tried an encouraging food grunt or two but the apes remained stationary.

Cohn thought they might eat if he left. "Tell them there's more where this came from," he said to Buz. "But please also say we'll have to be careful with distribution because the supply isn't endless. The way they stripped the baobab isn't advisable behavior. In fact, I urge them to be careful how much they eat once they get over their present pangs."

He reminded Buz to bring the basket back with him. He seemed to be admiring the young lady chimp, who now sat timidly at the very top of the tree.

Cohn, on leaving them, stepped behind a tall fern and peeked through it to watch the five chimpanzees climb down the tree in a single line and make for the basket with grunts, squeals, congratulatory back slappings and embraces. While four of them were hugging, the energetic male grabbed the basket and began to devour the red bananas. The rheumy old chimp approached him with extended palm, but the youthful ape, clutching the basket, would not part with even a banana skin.

Cohn was about to come thundering back but decided to let them work it out themselves. The husky one was obviously the dominant male and had certain privileges. Cohn would keep his eye on him to see that none of the others went hungry.

He returned to the cave and ate supper alone, a rice pudding with slices of tangerine baked into it. The food situation worried him. Would there be enough for all? Counting George, the island company now made eight. If eight, why not nine soon, or ten, enough for a hungry minyan?

He unfolded and examined his map of fruit trees. Bananas and figs were doing well; the figs would last at least eight weeks if the chimps were careful. Oranges and coconuts were plentiful, and so were dates, mangoes, and passion fruit. There was enough for all. Cohn thought he might apportion fruit trees so that each chimp would share what was available without trespassing on the rights of others.

And he was concerned what the unexpected appearance of five ape strangers might signify regarding God's decisive intent toward Calvin Cohn. Apparently He had slipped again, or was it His nature to be unable to count? Why should He have to if He contained all numbers, all possible combinations thereof? Or had He planned to develop it thus, individual animals appearing on the island, dribbling in one by one? For what purpose, if there was purpose?

After he had stopped posing himself unanswerable questions, Cohn stepped out of his cave, holding his kerosene lamp, to read in the evening cool. To his surprise, the visiting chimps—Buz among them—were sitting on the rocky ground in an untidy semicircle, as if expecting Cohn to walk over and officially greet them.

He wanted to, this was his chance to become acquainted. And he would take the occasion, after a word of welcome, to say how they could best get along together on this island.

"My dear primate brothers and sister," he began hoarsely. Cohn blew his nose before going on, when George the gorilla, his head helmeted with cockleburs, making him look like Mars himself if not a militant Moses or Joshua, emerged from the forest and cautiously beheld the assembled chimpanzees.

They, catching sight of the gorilla and the gigantic shadow he dragged after him, rose with excited hoots and shrieks and ran up the nearest trees.

When George observed Cohn's exasperated disappointment, he plunged into an empty cave and did not emerge for two days.

The five apes, perhaps tracking another basket of bananas, appeared at the cave again the next morning, but when Cohn came out in his lab apron, holding a leg bone of a fossilized ape he had been cleaning—screeching, the chimps galloped off and were at once in flight along arboreal ways.

Only the young female remained an instant, as if to satisfy a curiosity about the white-skinned ape before turning tail and flying off with the others.

Cohn was disappointed at not being able to establish contact with them. He looked forward to feeding them at his table. He hoped soon to set up rules and regulations for apportioning and distributing fruit. To have order you had to plan order. He had mentioned this to Buz and explained the American Constitution to him, asking him to convey his thoughts to the visiting apes. He wasn't sure of the range of ape comprehension, but given Buz's recent language experiences, held high hopes for them.

Buz assured him the chimps would understand more than he thought. "They know more thon you think they do. You hov to hov faith." Cohn decided to look further into the matter, so he changed into field boots and protective outer clothing, then pushed off into the rain forest in search of the newcomers.

After an unsuccessful morning, Cohn, on inspiration, came back to the woodland where some mango trees in full fruit grew, and there he found the migrant apes ensconced on a glossy-leaved tree, eating the sweet orange-yellow fruit, after trial bites having discarded dozens of stringy sour ones.

He was disappointed to see, as he approached them, that four of the six mango trees were already denuded of fruit, and the others would soon be. The ground was strewn with rotting fruit and yellow pits.

Cohn, standing under the mango where the apes squatted, addressed them in a cordial voice. "Brother and sister primates, welcome to this island; and if this is your native land, welcome anyway to our corner of this beautiful island."

"I hope you get the gist of what I am saying. If I didn't think that was possible, I wouldn't be standing here. In other words, I have faith." He listened for a smattering of applause but heard none.

"What I would hope you understand is the necessity of making a determined effort to learn a common tongue so that we can communicate with each other. Only if one knows the word, you might say, can he spread the word."

The chimps had stopped chewing and seemed to be absorbed in listening.

Cohn said he would like them to enjoy their stay, but if they intended to make this their place of permanent habitation, he sincerely hoped they would not mind a few observations concerning how certain matters might be arranged for everyone's mutual benefit.

"Calvin Cohn's my name, and I guess you can think of me as your protector, if you like the thought. I want you all to know I am not in the least interested in personal power; simply I would like to give the common effort a certain amount of reasonable direction."

He waited in vain for a random handclap. Cohn's voice fell a bit. "Take my word for it,

I would accept leadership reluctantly—my oceanographic colleagues used to say I had some talent for administration—however, I feel I ought to take responsibility because I've had a fairly decent education and perhaps a little more experience than most of you—to help establish what I hope will become an effective social community. Also I'm older than most of you, except maybe the old gentleman snoozing directly above me. Not that age is necessarily wisdom, but in certain ways it helps. Much, however, depends on the Lord."

Cohn laughed jovially, but when he beheld the two boys grinning in stupefaction, he told himself either shut up or be practical. He then addressed the multitude on the subject of food—that there would be enough around if they took care.

"Don't, for instance," Cohn seriously pleaded, "eat just to eat, or because you're bored. Kindly eat only when you're legitimately hungry, and then only enough to satisfy that hunger."

Someone in the tree let out a brash hoot whose source Cohn was unable to determine, but there was no other discourteous response to speak of.

"Please keep in mind that others have the right to share food sources equally, as free living beings. That's saying that freedom depends on mutual obligation, which is the bottom line, I'm sure you'll agree."

He heard petrified silence. After waiting for a change of heart, if that was the problem rather than their comprehension of his human language, Cohn felt he ought to shift his approach. "Let me tell you a story."

The apes seemed to lean forward in anticipation.

They understand, he thought excitedly, and went at once into an old tale of a chimpanzee named Leopold, an absentminded gentleman, somewhat a narcissist, who ate without thought of other chimps' natural rights, until he ate himself into such swollen proportions that, swallowing one last grape, he burst.

Dead silence.

They must know that one, Cohn reflected. Either that or they don't like the way it ended. He asked if there were any questions, and nobody had one.

Wanting to do it better—get it right—Cohn began another story, about someone he knew who fasted days at a time so he could feed poor people who had nothing at all to eat.

This man's wife asked, "How will you give them what you don't eat, if we have nothing to eat anyway?"

"God will take nothing from me and give something to them," said the old rabbi.

Cohn asked if they had got the point of the story.

But the stunned apes were no longer listening. A stream of dung from where the dominant male stood barely missed Cohn's head.

An explosion of derisive sounds filled the dense mango, and the apes, one by one, dropped out of its branches and disappeared into the woodland.

Cohn made no attempt to follow them. Either they hadn't liked his stories, or his language had failed to communicate anything but a monotonous voice. In afterthought he felt it was perhaps overambitious to have hit them with so many new concepts.

He felt that these apes lacked Buz's gifts of communication and wondered if he could learn, by rereading Dr. Bünder's notebooks, how he had performed the laryngeal operation on Buz. Yet what good would the operation itself be if there were no electronic voice boxes to install?

Vaguely stirred, vaguely dissatisfied, Cohn hurried back to his cave and began to draw up plans for a heavy gate for the entrance, but search where he would, could find no strong metal pin to hang it on.

He began instead to construct a wall of split oak logs—very hard work—a device he planned to put on rollers so it could quickly be moved across the mouth of the cave in case of peril.

Since the arrival of the five chimps, Buz

had made himself comparatively scarce at the cave. Reasonably enough—he liked hanging out with his new friends, understandable for a creature who had been deprived of a carefree childhood.

Once a week, or twice, he came in for supper with his dod and stayed over. Or he came to hear a story. For months he had asked only for Cain and Abel. "Thot's where the oction is." Once in a while he returned for a swig of banana beer and then was out again till all hours.

One pre-dawn night Cohn woke from a stark dream of drowning, hearing gurgling sounds. He feared another flood but then remembered Buz's borborygmus.

In the dark he could hear the chimp stealthily picking through the food stores for some morsel or other. Outside, the sky lit up in foggy flashes of summer lightning.

Cohn aimed his torch at Buz, who instinctively bristled when the light hit him. He self-consciously climbed down the shelf.

"I hope you aren't monkeying with my phonograph records?" Cohn said.

"I om not a monkey," said Buz. "Ond I don't eat voice records like some stupid gorillas do. Whot I om looking for is a piece of coconut condy for Mary Modelyn."

"Who's Mary Madelyn?"

"The girl chimponzee I om interested in."

"Did you give her that name?"

Buz proudly said he had. He said naming was nobody's monopoly.

Cohn said it had been Adam's task and on this island was his. "But I have no objection if you name a few names—if you kindly notify me first."

Buz said he didn't see why he had to. Naming names was freedom of speech. Cohn dropped the subject, not wanting to inhibit him.

"Are you romantically interested in her?"

"Thot depends. Om I sexuolly moture enough yet?"

"That's for you to say, Buz. Some male chimps are slower than others. Some attempt to mount a female when they are eight or nine months old."

"I hod nobody to mount when I was thot age, not even my mother to proctice on."

Cohn told him not to worry, he'd get the swing of it when he had to.

"Not with thot loudmouth Esau around. He growls when he sees me looking at her. He's two years post my age and hos strong muscles."

"Is Esau the aggressive male? Did you name him too?"

"He's the hairy ape. I hov named all the new ones."

Cohn wanted to know the other names.

"Melchoir is the old one."

"Named for whom?"

"Dr. Bünder's father-in-law. He used to give me marshmollows."

"Who else?"

"Luke and Saul of Tarsus are twins."

"Where did you get their names?"

"Dr. Bünder had two gerbils with those names."

Cohn got out of bed, slipped on his robe, and they sat in their rockers facing each other. He asked Buz if the apes were a family, and Buz replied they had met in their wanderings on the island after the Flood.

"Where did they stay during the Flood?"

Buz said he didn't know, probably in trees. He said that Mary Madelyn liked Melchior and got along with the twins, but not with Esau. "All he wants is sex."

"Won't she oblige?"

"She hosn't yet but con't guorontee whot might hoppen ofter she goes into heat. She says she would prefer me as a lover if I hurried my development."

"You're almost there."

The cave was lit by light flashes in the sky.

"Whot's thot?" Buz asked nervously.

Cohn explained it was heat lightning, also nothing to worry about. "It's caused by a discharge of atmospheric electricity traveling from one cloud to another."

"Why don't I know thot?"

Cohn admitted he had never told him and guessed neither had Dr. Bünder. "I can't tell you every fact I know."

Buz said he had every right to know what was going on in the world without asking the human race.

Cohn replied there wasn't much of the human race on the island. "But if you stayed home nights and paid more attention to your reading, instead of fantasizing when you can begin to have sexual relations, you'd pick up a lot of useful information about the world around us."

Buz said he had his own life to live and would live it as he saw fit.

Cohn, feeling Buz had become snappish lately, which he attributed to the approach of puberty, wouldn't argue with that. He did say he was concerned about getting the new chimps organized and living by the law of the island.

"Whot law is thot?"

"A law we'll have to put together—all of us—but it won't work unless we can communicate with one another. That means speech. Maybe we ought to begin teaching these recently arrived chimps a sign language. You know Ameslan, and I know a little, and if we can persuade them to show up for language lessons, we can teach them several signs a day. That's at least a beginning."

Buz then sprang an astonishing surprise. "I hov already taught the new chimponzees to speak the English longuoge and hoven't only been fontasying sexuol relations."

"You have what?" Cohn said in amazement. "Is it possible?"

"It is more than possible, it is on occomplished foct."

Cohn felt an overwhelming elation. Apologizing for his previous invidious remark, he kindled the lamp and drew the ivy curtain. When the night was warm he kept the ivy tied in bunches at the sides of the cave opening.

Long shadows whirled on the walls.

"But how can they talk if they have no apparatus for speech?" Cohn asked in a whisper, "no adequate larynx?"

"Their speech is not os well articulated os mine, but they hov ocquired longuoge because they hov faith."

"In whom and what?"

"In whot I hov told them."

"What was that?"

"Thot they could learn if they hod faith."

"Incredible," Cohn muttered. "A stupendous miracle if it has really occurred."

Buz insisted it had. Unusual things were abroad on the island. "Fruit is more abundont and sweeter this season. I heard mogic strains of music in those winding caves we found—prettier music thon you play on thot voice mochine. Ond now my friends hov learned to talk by an oct of faith. If you hov faith you con hear them talk."

Cohn humbly said he hod faith.

* * *

Though Cohn, as scientist, could not explain how the chimps had learned to speak English, he was of course gratified that they had learned. If explanation was needed: the world was different from once it was; and what might happen, and what could not, he was not as sure of as he used to be. It seemed to him that after a frightening period of incoherence, there was now a breath of settled purpose in the universe. One could not say for sure where the Almighty stood after the Second Flood; but if He had permitted the visiting chimps to learn one of the languages unique to homo sapiens—had allowed them to go on living through Devastation and Flood in order to learn—one might say—why not similar good grace for Cohn?

In celebration of the miraculous descent, or spontaneous emergence of human speech among the apes, he planned a seder. Cohn figured that the fifteenth day of Nisan had gone its way, but since there were no calendars available, one could not be held responsible for exact dates.

It wasn't, anyway, the date that counted, it was the mood and purpose of the occasion: simply a celebration—nothing extraordinary—a means of bringing together the island company, and at the same time politely thanking Someone for favors received. Nothing wrong with a little sincere gratitude for every amelioration of an unforgivable condition caused by the Creator. He had his problems too. After all, First Causes were not always first causes; and maybe He was having second thoughts about these matters.

Anyway, it was a beautiful early spring. The bright green grass was ankle-high. Fragrant flowers, astonishing ones, were scattered everywhere. Mimosas were abloom in flaring yellow. Oleander was white and bougainvillea royal purple. Each color seemed deeper, more livingly intense, than its ordinary color. It seemed a splendid year ahead. Peace to all, amen.

Cohn diligently cleaned the cave, swept, shined, mopped. And he had built a long teak table that would seat eight—three on each side bench, one at head and foot.

He carried out and hid, according to ritual, all suspected unleavened food, recalling how his mother, holding a candle in her hand, had prayed on this occasion, "May all the leaven in my possession, whether I have seen it or not, be annulled and considered as dust of the earth." In those days dust of the earth was a more innocent substance.

Cohn was the official host and Buz assisted. The guests were the five new chimps, and George the gorilla, if he was in the mood to appear. Any way one looked at it, the gorilla was a permanent inhabitant of the island and had to be encouraged to join the company. Cohn had more or less forgiven him for destroying his father's record—"Kol Nidre," nothing less, a sad loss—probably George had thought the record was a licorice wafer or something equally good to eat.

To invite him personally, since there were no mail deliveries, and since Buz wouldn't go in his place to persuade him to attend, Cohn scouted George's usual haunts. He came across his nests in the flattened deep grass but rarely found a trace of George himself, not even a fragment of fibrous dung where he had recently made camp. Gorillas soiled their nests but were not themselves soiled; chimps, because of their liquid excrement, would tend to perform their bowel functions outside their nests, and save himself who loitered below. Who was, therefore, the more civilized?

Buz said that probably the giant ape's fear of the presence of six lively chimpanzees had scared him away.

Cohn replied George would be welcome if he came. "I'll put him down for Elijah's seat, but whoever sits there first is the guest of honor."

"Not thot fot ape, in the cave I live in."

"This is a celebration. Be generous, Buz."

"I om but I om not cuckoo. You don't like thot monster any more thon I do. You said thot ofter he smoshed your father's music record."

"I've since had second thoughts. Frankly,

I respect him. I feel there's more than gorilla to George."

"Yes, he is bigger and stupider."

"He is a lonely ape. I sense he's had a bad time beyond our late bad times, perhaps a personal crisis. He may look fierce but has a gentle heart. I suspect he was the one who helped me when I was sick with radiation poisoning. And keep in mind that he never had your advantages, Buz."

Buz covered his nose with one hand and tugged at an imaginary toilet chain with the other hand. He could have got the gesture only from Dr. Bünder.

Seder night was a night of full moon. Wearing a reasonable facsimile of a traditional white kitl he had stitched together out of a roll of mosquito netting they had fetched from the hold of the *Rebekah Q*, Cohn prepared the festive seder meal. He had baked a batch of thin, round, crisp flatcakes, according to the tradition of the hastily baked bread in Exodus.

Cohn covered the teak table with a portion of sail they had recovered from the former oceanographic schooner. Since they had only one candle left, he installed the lit kerosene lamp as centerpiece; and in the shadowy scene on the cave wall the seated chimps looked like wise elders.

On the teak table stood two slender-necked blue vases Cohn had recently potted out of some rare lumps of clay, aburst with white fruit-tree blossoms he had painted on them. And there were three carafes of banana wine, a tasty light wine, something like a gewürztraminer, that required a longer fermentation than the fizzy banana beer.

For baked eggs—nothing on the island could lay an egg—he served pickled red palm nuts. A platter of matzos lay on the table covered with a linen napkin. Instead of bitter herbs Cohn offered cut-up chunks of cassava root.

In place of lamb shankbone, he had served on each wooden plate a portion of leg bone of a fossil he was almost certain was Eohippus, the fox-size, dawn horse, the first of this species to be discovered outside North America. Cohn, in tense excitement, had dug up the leg bone, embedded in limestone, in a backyard dig in the field beyond the rice paddy. The bone, hardly kosher, and expendable because he already had two hind right-leg femurs in his bone box—was for ritual purposes only; to be used symbolically, therefore he hoped permissibly. Eohippus, if that's what it was, suited the occasion because it was distantly related to the thundering equi of the Egyptian charioteers.

Mary Madelyn picked up her small portion of bone and cautiously sniffed it; she hastily replaced it on the plate.

"For symbolic use only, not for eating," Cohn explained in a whisper, patting her hand, and she, affectionate creature, patted his.

Instead of haroset, he served a sweet paste of chopped apricots and nuts from a ten-pound bag they had found in the vessel. For lettuce and celery, he placed a small bouquet of oak leaves on the plate before each chimp. For himself he had collected a few rice shoots that reminded him of a Japanese drawing he had once owned.

And for the ritual red wine he poured white banana wine into the rough wooden tumblers he had carved. Bit by bit Cohn was replacing objects he and Buz had salvaged with ones he made himself. Each tumbler depicted an epic scene from Exodus of the escape of the Israelites from their Egyptian oppressors—the symbolic escape that dwelt in the minds of Jews throughout history and inspired them in times of desperation. On his own tumbler Cohn had portrayed the visage of Moshe Rebbenu, with his two-pronged beard. One might have mistaken it for the likeness of God himself, if that was possible.

Cohn sat at the head of the table, opposite the cave entrance, facing the empty seat for Elijah, or whoever appeared in his place. Here he could easily reach to the fireplace ledge where he had baked the matzos and prepared the food.

The appearance of the visiting chimps had improved. Their hair had grown in and their coats were sleek. They were energetic and talkative. Cohn enjoyed hearing them talk among themselves.

On the bench to his right sat trusty Buz; next to him, Melchior; and to his side Saul of Tarsus, whom the old man kept a wet eye on.

On his left, Cohn had seated Mary Madelyn, at her request opposite Buz and as far from Esau as she could be; not very far, for only Luke sat between them. Esau tended to make a nuisance of himself although she tried not to notice each offense. Buz, however, bristled. The situation between the two young apes was charged, and Cohn tried to keep them busy with ritual.

Melchior, the graybeard chimp, oversaw the twins on both sides of the table. What they did not eat on their plates or drink from their cups, he willingly consumed.

Mary Madelyn was an intelligent, attractive young female with silken hair, a somewhat heart-shaped, healthy face—a trifle pale—and an affectionate manner. Her sexy ears lay close to the head. She had almost a real figure, Cohn thought. When Melchior grew too sleepy to fuss over the restive twins, a glance from her would calm them.

Cohn began the seder with a kiddush for wine, and the first two toasts he proposed were the traditional ones to life and to freedom.

Closing his eyes, he recited, "Our thanks to God who kept us alive and sustained us to this moment"—(notwithstanding the fact He had not sustained any others, ran through Cohn's mind, but he banished the thought. Not on this night of celebration).

When he explained who God was everyone at the table cheered.

Buz tugged at Cohn's kitl. "I thought you told me He let the Holocaust ond Second Flood hoppen?"

"I'm thanking Him for what good He did, not for what He did badly," Cohn whispered. "You and I are alive, as are those present, despite the Devastation. Certain grateful thanks therefore are due to Whom they are due. That's how I look at it."

Buz crossed himself and the twins followed suit; they imitated him often.

"Do that later, Buz," Cohn said sotto voce.

"Whot's wrong with now?"

"It's not part of this ceremony. It's another modality."

Buz took a moment to memorize the word and went on eating.

Cohn lifted his tumbler and toasted peace. "Next year on this blessed isle—may we all have prospered!"

"I hope we hov freedom of religion," Buz said.

"Amen," said Cohn, toasting every freedom.

All joined the toast and drank down the banana wine. Buz went around the table refilling the tumblers. Esau tried to trip him but Buz hopped over his foot. Though his hair had risen he kept out of a fight. Mary Madelyn smiled at him.

Cohn knew he wasn't following the sequence of the seder, but what counted was the spirit, and that was running high.

He had explained that the seder was originally a Passover celebration. "The Jews were slaves in Egypt and God brought them out. That's the thing to keep in mind, that He brought them out, although not always quickly enough in the recent past. In any case, tonight we are celebrating the escape from Egypt and our own personal escape from the Second Flood, though our burden of mourning is still heavy. Our present ceremony is also a thanksgiving for our life on this island. We're alive and in good health. Our task is to co-exist peacefully in the future."

Buz crossed himself and Cohn pretended not to notice.

Melchior and Mary Madelyn clapped their hands in approval of his little homily. Cohn hoped he hadn't bored them. Esau was trying to blow bubbles with his banana wine. The twins giggled.

But the ceremony flowed on pleasurably. Then came the Four Questions. Since neither of the twins could be depended on to stay with the script—Saul of Tarsus seemed slightly autistic; he spoke one word at a time after breathy pauses, yet he knuckle-walked steadily, if clumsily, and brachiated boldly; and Luke seemed to lack power of concentration—Cohn had asked Buz to ask the questions.

Cohn had primed him concerning the seder. He had also composed the questions to elicit as much information as possible about the visiting chimps, hoping to understand the Lord's purpose in letting them live after the Flood.

These were the questions:

1. Assuming the proposition is correct, how does this night differ from all others?

2. Please state who you are, that is to say, define yourself.

3. Do you know where you were born? What were your experiences during the Second Flood? How did you save yourself from the rising water?

4. Do you think of life as having a particular purpose? What is it? Please answer responsively.

Cohn had hand-printed the questions, and Buz, now seriously into reading, had memorized them before eating the printed page. He loved the taste of paper. Once in a rare while Cohn gave him a blank notebook sheet for a confection.

Seeming to relish his role as correspondent, Buz recited each question, and Melchior and Mary Madelyn volunteered to answer them. Esau announced that the questions were stupid but he would respond because he had nothing better to do.

Since acquiring speech, he had developed into a self-important overweight ape trying hard to resemble a gorilla. His face was large, his teeth unsettled and wandering in the mouth. Yet he enunciated quite clearly and spoke without hesitation. His eyes were restless, his expression, challenging. Buz obviously disliked and feared him. Esau seemed not to fear anyone and to dislike all.

Cohn considered him a bright-enough chimp, not without native wit, but surely a case of arrested emotional development. He had made up his mind to have a serious talk with him. Esau threatened; he rocked the boat.

Esau declared he would answer first. Buz asked each question forthrightly, yet modestly, and Esau proclaimed his replies.

"For question 1, all nights are the same except when it's raining, or I am having dirty thoughts." He made the sound of a kiss to Mary Madelyn, and she, dear lady, pretended she was hard of hearing.

"For question 2, I am the Alpha Ape of us all. And that's a warning to stay away from my girl."

He stared fixedly at Buz, who, after glancing at Cohn, drank from his tumbler of wine, and asked the next question.

"For 3," said Esau, "I don't remember where I was born. My mother used to say I had made myself out of mud and water. At the time of the high water I climbed to the top of a palm tree, lived on the coconuts, and crapped in the Flood till it ran off."

Cohn asked him not to be tasteless, there was a lady present.

"On the fourth question, my answer is short. My purpose in my life right at this particular time is to slip it to Mary Madelyn as soon as she learns the facts of life. She doesn't know what she is missing."

Mary Madelyn blushed deeply.

"Don't spoil the seder," Cohn warned Esau. "We're expecting Elijah."

Buz whispered in his ear that they would have to get rid of the brute, but Cohn replied they had to have faith. "We can't reject him at first whiff."

He thanked Esau for his frank replies and called Melchior.

Bored when the old ape rose to answer the Four Questions, Esau gnawed on the Eohippus bone. It turned to dust in his mouth. He spat it out with a gasping cough and gurgled down a carafe of wine. In a few minutes he was soundly asleep at the table. No one waked him.

Melchior cleared his throat and warmed up his breathy voice. His speech was slurpy—every word swam in spittle, but he spoke slowly and could be understood. The old ape had trouble breathing and would bang his chest with his fist to move air into his lungs.

He answered thus: "One to two—the weather is dry and I feel fine, thank you. Whether it's day or night I don't think about nowadays." He wheezed wetly, his eyes turning slightly milky. "I feel a heaviness of the chesht but that's the way of age. My mother used to say we exchange ailments for yearzh. We take on one as we give up the other. It doesn't pay to live too long in my theory. Thank you kindly.

"On question 3," he said, "what's that again?"

Buz repeated it.

"One day I woke up in a tree nesht with my mother. She was good to me till the day she went off with a gentleman she had met. I followed them in the foresht and then got losht and did not ever find her again. I will miss her till the end of my days—which is not too far off."

Cohn remarked there was time enough to think of death.

"No time at all," said Melchior with an extended wheeze.

"The fourth question," Cohn reminded him, "concerns purpose in life."

"I have no regretsh," said Melchior.

Cohn said he hadn't told them how he had escaped the Flood.

"I found a big shnow mountain and sat on it eating leaves until the water on the land below disappeared. Then I began to vomit and losht all my hair. I looked like a newborn babe. I was ashamed of my nakedness, but I climbed down off the mountain and went to the lowlands. Your fruit is delicious in this country. Please don't anyone hurt me. I am a pretty old ape."

Cohn said he had forbidden strife. "This is a peaceful island."

"We hov forbidden strife," Buz said.

"Everybody wovs you," Mary Madelyn said to Melchior.

Whenever she pronounced an el it became doubleu. Buz giggled but Cohn liked the sound of it.

The twins cheered Melchior. That woke Esau, gagging. He was about to throw up over the tablecloth, but Cohn got him out of the cave in time. "Horseass," groaned Esau as he retched in the bushes.

Cohn left him there and returned to the cave to serve a platter of bananas flambé, with slices of boiled apricots stewed in brandy, their last bottle from the wreck. All ate heartily.

Then Mary Madelyn answered the questions. Except for her partial lallation she spoke well, though not as fluently as Buz, who, despite the fact he had initiated it, seemed jealous of her swift progress in language.

Cohn had read her the balcony scene from *Romeo and Juliet,* and though she hardly understood every word, she had listened raptly.

She had told Cohn she didn't know her age but suspected she would soon be old enough to bear a child.

"Do you look forward to it?"

"Yes, but not to be in estrus."

"Why not?"

"It's humiwiating to present mysewf every time a mawe approaches. I wish to be independent and free."

"Have you ever been in heat?"

"Pwease," Mary Madelyn said, "I don't wike that word; in fact I detest it. No, I have never been in estrus."

Cohn begged her pardon. "I know how you feel."

Mary Madelyn looked at him with a doubtful smile. She confessed she was afraid of Esau. "He threatens me by shaking big branches in my face and caws me awfuw names. He said he would break my behind if I keep on being sexuawy off-putting."

"How do you handle that?"

"I asked him to wait for my fuw natuaw devewopment."

"Then what happens?"

She said she was afraid to think.

She was an altogether interesting lady chimpanzee. Cohn thought she would look lovely in a white dress, but where would you shop for one nowadays?

Mary Madelyn then responded to the Four Questions:

"Yes, this night is different because we are

cewebrating our survivaw now that the wicked water has run off and the vomiting sickness is no wonger in us."

"Bravo," Cohn said.

Buz nudged his arm with his head. "When do I hov my turn to onswer?"

"Tonight is your turn to ask and others to answer."

"I would rother onswer than osk," Buz said.

"Not tonight," said Cohn.

Esau, looking as though he had lost five pounds, had knuckle-walked back into the cave and taken his seat on the bench. He smelled of vomit but none of the chimps save Buz seemed to mind. He privately held his nose.

"I am the best answerer," Esau announced. "I am King of the Trees."

"I think Mr. Mewchior is," said Mary Madelyn.

The twins applauded and Melchior, tentatively chewing a matzo, nodded.

"And you are a bitch-whore," Esau spoke across the table.

She slid as far from him as she could. Another inch and she would be sitting in Cohn's lap—not wise for decorum.

"In answer to the second question," she said, "my name is Mary Madewyn, a femawe chimpanzee who respects hersewf and wishes to be respected by others."

"Beautiful," commented Cohn.

"You praise her but never praise me," Buz complained in a whisper.

Cohn whispered she was their guest. "The third question?" he asked.

"First there was the Fwood and then came the awfuw nights of rain. We wost our poor mother in the rising water before we cwimbed to the headwands. After the Fwood sank, my baby sister and I were sick in a wet cave. She died there and I weft and wandered on, miserabwy awone untiw I met Mr. Mewchior and the twins.

"When Esau joined our group he said he was our weader. He got wost wherever we went, and Mr. Mewchior had to show us the way. Soon we came to this wand of fruit trees and decided to stay. Buz found us and taught us to speak your wanguage. He towd us his dod was a white chimpanzee, and no one bewieved it untiw we met you."

"God's grace," said Cohn.

"As for question 4," Mary Madelyn went on, "my speciew purpose in wife is to wiv."

"Marvelously put," he said.

Buz produced a mild rumble with his lips not unlike that which Cohn in his boyhood had known as a Bronx cheer. And Esau gurgled as if he was swallowing a whole egg, but it was the way he laughed.

No one asked questions of the twins.

"We are too young," said Luke.

Saul of Tarsus nodded sagely.

Cohn removed the napkin from the matzo

bowl. "This is the bread of affliction," he recited. "Let us eat to remember who we are."

"Who are we?" Buz said, despite himself, asking.

"The still-alive—those who have survived despite the terrible odds," Cohn said. He passed a matzo to each of them except Melchior, who slowly chewed the broken piece he held in his hand. The chimps bit into the unleavened bread and spat it out, except Buz, who was used to the taste. He got his matzo down with a fistful of oak leaves and a long drink of banana wine. Mary Madelyn politely nibbled hers in tiny bites.

Cohn began the singing—"A Kid for Two Farthings." Though he urged them all to join no one would, so he put on a record of his father the cantor chanting "Chad Gadye" in a way that made the apes dance.

They danced at the rear of the cave and watched their shadows dance. The twins chased after the dancing shadows, slapping the wall with their palms.

At the end of the seder, Cohn poured a tumbler of wine to toast Elijah the Prophet.

The cantor was singing: "God is Almighty . . . / Awesome is His mystery."

The chimps at the table were grooming one another. Esau insisted on combing Mary Madelyn's rump, as she groomed Buz. Luke picked among the hairs of Saul of Tarsus's head, and Saul did the same for Luke. Cohn was wondering whether—to be congenial—

he ought to groom himself, when a streak of light flashed across the rear wall of the cave as George the gorilla, sweeping aside the ivy curtain, eased himself into the chamber.

A heavy, nose-filling odor of bay leaves and garlic seeped into the cave as he paused at the entrance to stare at the assemblage of apes at the table.

Cohn at once rose to welcome the visitor and offered him Elijah's seat.

The chimps, grinning in fear, froze in their places.

Cohn urged them all to remain calm. "This is a different night. Nobody wants to harm anybody. It's a night of peace and a celebration of life. Sit down, George, and have a glass of wine."

George, sitting bulkily at the table, drank from a tumbler of banana wine. He sat with eyes lowered as if to affirm he was their peaceful neighbor. To prove it he smiled, revealing his fangs.

The chimps slid to the ends of both benches close to Cohn. Even Esau had gone pale.

Cohn asked George to taste his matzo and say a good word to his friends-and-fellow-islanders.

The giant ape, after a hesitant bite he seemed to relish, strove to speak. He coughed, strained, sighed. His throat bulged. Now he grunted as though resisting constipation. His heavy black form trembled as if he was feverish. In desperation, George rose from the chair and beat his booming chest. The cave resounded loudly with the drumming. With a roar of rage he lifted and overturned the teak table. Ths seder food and wine crashed to the floor.

The shrieking, hooting chimpanzees scattered. They rushed out of the cave into the night and hastily disappeared in every direction.

Cohn's father was singing a hymn in praise of deliverance.

George, slumped in Elijah's chair, listened, moodily munching his matzo.

Cohn, although outraged by the shambles the gorilla had made of the seder—their first communal enterprise—restrained his anger, in keeping with the spirit of the evening, and even attempted to cheer up the unfortunate ape. For as long as he lived on the island there could be no functioning community without George. Outsiders were dangerous; he had to be in.

"George," said Cohn, "for certain reasons I forgive you the mess you made tonight at the end of an unusual occasion, and while I'm forgiving I want you to know I no longer hold it against you that you absconded with, and destroyed, a rare record of my father's. But I have to tell you this: either change your ways or go your way."

George, after a moment of depressed silence, moaned.

Cohn, on impulse, asked the gorilla the

Four Questions and, not surprisingly, got no reply. He then related the story of the Prodigal Son, a parable Buz had more than once requested, and the gorilla listened with tears flowing as he consumed large pieces of damp matzo.

"They that sow in tears," sang the passionate cantor, "shall reap in joy."

"Amen," answered Cohn.

George bonged his chest in joy.

After he had swept the cave and put things away, Cohn, as he slept, conceived a white dream. An albino ape had appeared in the mist-laden forest, a fearsome male chimpanzee no one had seen but all seemed to know of.

"Is he for real?" Cohn asked Buz, and Buz replied, "He hos to be, I dream of him often."

Cohn lived in serious concern that the white ape might appear in his cave and make demands. He foresaw trouble.

He felt he would not be at ease until he had talked with the creature, asked who he was, and what he wanted here. If he wished to join the community, let him sign up.

One morning he set out to find the albino ape in the rain forest. He remained there searching for three days and nights, but got no more than a muffled glimpse of a white figure, dimly lit amid misty trees and the green-gloomy foliage.

Exasperated, Cohn flung his iron spear (he had chanced on it in the *Rebekah Q)* to the ground; and in his dream was angered at God for having got him to this island and into this dream. "What kind of God is that?"

At once, above the trees, he beheld a bulbous cloud shaped like a white tulip held aloft by strains of music.

Mr. Cohn? an angelic voice spoke, one so beautiful that Cohn was all goose pimples when he heard it. He sank to his knees. "Yes, sir, or ma'am, whichever the case may be."

Mr. Cohn, please don't utter blasphemous thoughts. Or express childish doubts about the Deity. I say this for your good.

Cohn sincerely apologized. "I'm sorry I misspoke. After seeing that white ape, I felt a dread something bad might happen."

State the nature of that dread.

"Was he really there like a dim light in those trees, or is it all imagined and dreamed by me?"

He is insofar as it seems to be, said the angelic voice.

Cohn groaned at length. "That moldy chestnut encore?"

What there is to use we use, the angel replied.

"What I want to know is: Is he on this island, and others like him in black or brown? Or any like me?" Cohn went on, "Another human being, for instance—perhaps female—anywhere in what's left of the world?

I wish to know for my peace of mind. Put yourself in my place."

Where I put myself is not your concern, Mr. Cohn. But I will say in answer to your question that there are none like you anywhere, any more.

"How would anybody know for sure?"

Who knows anything for sure?

"That old saw, too?"

What's usable we use, said the angel with the beautiful voice.

"Then who knows what's happening anywhere? Is this island what it seems to be?"

What does it seem to be?

"At least an island with two on it, conversing."

Whatever I reply, would you in reality believe me?

"Not necessarily," Cohn warily said.

So call it a dream.

"No more than that?" he cried.

But the angel had gone, though the haunting sound of his voice lingered.

Cohn woke holding his spear aloft in a dark-green forest.

He feared God more than he loved Him.

How can I square it with Him for that dream I think I dreamed, if that's what it was, assuming He knows? He must, it is His Name and Nature. I've got to be careful.

It seemed to Cohn he had to be wary, indeed, in dealing with God. Theoretically no, but in truth yes. He was constantly slipping up, speaking and acting in error against his best interests; not containing his dissatisfactions; not therefore protecting himself, considering his hunger to survive.

I have to watch my words, also thoughts and dreams.

They had irreconcilable differences concerning whose responsibility the Day of Devastation was. Cohn still had trouble subduing his rage and grief therefrom; but practically speaking, the event was beyond redoing and one had the future to contend with.

In that matter the Lord held every card in His comprehensive hand; and if Cohn held one it was invisible to him, except perhaps his extraordinary knowledge that God did not know everything. *He* had difficulty with numbers, could not always count accurately; for instance, there were more than only poor Cohn alive on earth. That was the only card Cohn held.

Still if he wanted to go on breathing on this less-than-perfect, magic island, as indeed he did if it was at all feasible, he had to invent some practical means of winning God's favor while not exactly taking Him off the hook for perpetrating His Latest Flood.

Cohn hoped the Lord had appreciated his seder and all the nice things they had said about Him the other night.

* * *

What might please God would be some sensible arrangement of the lives of the apes on the island into a functioning social community, interacting lives; and with Cohn as advisor and protector to help them understand themselves and fulfill the social contract. Maybe start with a sort of small family and extend into community? You are not the chimps your fathers were—you can talk. Yours, therefore, is the obligation to communicate, speak as equals, work and together build, evolve into concerned, altruistic living beings.

Not bad if it worked. How would Cohn know unless and until he tried? On this island more seemed possible than one might imagine. A functioning social unit, even as small as seven or eight living beings, would be a civilizing force inspiring a higher order of behavior—to a former lower order of creatures—highest now that man was more or less kaput.

If this small community behaved, developed, endured, it might someday—if some chimpy Father Abraham got himself born—produce its own Covenant with God. So much better for God, Who seemed to need one to make Him feel easy with Himself as Party-of-the-First-Part, even though He found it troublesome, in the long run, to make the Covenant work as it should. One could hardly look after the party of the second part every minute of the day.

It was better to attempt to civilize whoever needed civilizing, the Lord would surely agree—more good that way, less evil. A good society served a good purpose; He would surely approve if Cohn dedicated himself to fostering it.

To do what God might be expecting, now that a common language existed between himself and the chimps, Cohn felt he ought to try to educate them up to some decent level, eventually to make them aware of the cosmos and of mankind, too, who had fallen from earth and cosmos, because men had failed each other in obligations and responsibilities—failed to achieve brotherhood, lost their lovely world, not to mention living lives.

Therefore Cohn established a schooltree for them, a bushy-leaved, bark-peeled, hard-blue-acorned eucalyptus tree exuding a nose-opening aromatic odor, especially after rain, that kept them alert in the grove of mixed trees, some of which were crabbed live oaks not more than sixty feet from his cave.

The apes, including Buz, who was advanced in schooling but liked to listen to others being taught, attended classes regularly, spending two hours each morning getting educated; except on the Seventh Day, when Cohn preferred not to teach because, since he did not keep track of time, he might inadvertently be working on the Sabbath. God was a great fan of the Sabbath, and it was worth anybody's life, it said in Exodus, to work on that day.

So he skipped each Seventh Day to show his respect and good will.

Cohn blew on a brass horn to summon them to class.

The apes, some reluctantly, climbed the eucalyptus and moved out on spreading limbs of the blowsy tree, sitting alone or in two's, chewing leaves and spitting them out; or cracking nuts they had brought along, and eating them out of their palms as they listened to Calvin Cohn lecture; or groomed themselves and their partners as he droned on. When the lectures got to be boring they would shake branches and throw nuts at him. They hooted and grunted, but subsided when Cohn raised his hand, indicating he intended to do better.

He sat on a stool he had assembled at the foot of the shedding schooltree, on a leaf-covered hillock of hard earth he had constructed as a teaching platform, talking fast or slow, depending on the subject. He addressed them on a variety of topics, or inspired thoughts, formally or casually; or he read aloud from one book or another. And Cohn related tales he had made up as best he could the night before as he prepared his lectures; or had culled from memory.

He was no Martin Buber and the apes no Hasidim, though they might someday be, Cohn permitted himself to think. These things needed time. It depended, to some degree, on how one addressed the apes and they played it back.

The chimps seemed, on the whole, to enjoy their schooling although there were occasional truants, Esau, for instance, a prime offender; and Luke and Saul of Tarsus, after a difficult lesson had left them dazed, usually took the next day off. Melchior was steady, he liked to listen; and so did Mary Madelyn, who discreetly applauded certain things Cohn said and some he only hinted at.

Buz, diligently present, sometimes interrupted the teacher's discourse to disagree with a fact. He also corrected Cohn's mistakes in usage, when he caught a "which" for a "that," or "precipitate" for "precipitous." Buz had been immersed in dictionary study lately. Cohn, when corrected, felt some embarrassment, especially when the other chimps broke out in applause for Buz. However, the amateur teacher—he so defined himself—was good-humored about his little errors, and education went on.

George the gorilla was a part-time scholar, listening from a neighboring cedar, because the apes, particularly after the seder shambles, showed they did not care to have him among them. George could tell and had picked himself this tall coniferous tree twenty feet from the eucalyptus. Cohn argued with the chimps, defending the gorilla's human rights, but fortunately George preferred to be by himself.

He crouched on the lower branch of the cedar, at times lay outstretched, chewing a weed, seemingly absorbed in Cohn's remarks and stories, though one never knew for sure because the gorilla did not talk; yet Cohn was almost certain he comprehended what he heard.

However, his attention to the lesson appeared to be fitful, partly because he seemed to be roused, or struck, by certain things, and for a while was not able to concentrate on anything more. At least it seemed so to Cohn.

George would stay in his tree until some interesting fact, or quotation, or tale, excited his fancy, at which moment he lowered himself to the ground and went reeling off into the forest as though high on reflection, to hoots of ridicule by the students in the schooltree. Cohn pictured him lying in the sun-warmed grass, playing with a thought till it arranged itself in his head. Or was that giving the beast more credit than he deserved? Yet there was something "possible" about George. He looked like himself plus something else he might be.

After the daily lectures, the chimps climbed down the eucalyptus to enjoy a cup of fizzy banana beer that Cohn served to all present.

Melchior, as he guzzled the beer dripping into his beard, stopped drinking long enough to say this was the besht part of the day.

Cohn thought he knew more about fossils than anything else he had studied, but with the help, if not collaboration, of his one-volume encyclopedia he would try to inform them about the major doings of the past.

"Knowing what occurred in the world might favor the future. Yours, I mean, rather than mine. Mine looks scarce; yours, at least possible."

He said, "There are gaps in my knowledge, large and small, but I will tell it as best I can. If you listen, there may be some morsels to nibble on. I sincerely hope you won't think I am being reductive."

The chimps in the eucalyptus, with the exception of sour-faced Esau, who sat on his hairy hands, politely applauded Cohn's honest declaration.

So in the days that followed he lectured on the cosmos—from Big Bang to Dying Whimper of man (for whom Cohn asked, and got, a full minute's silence). The apes were curious about practically everything that had happened on earth and heaven. Starting there, the universe expanded.

"What for?" asked Buz.

"Because it's expansible."

(Laughter.)

He detailed Descent, Advent, Ascent of Man, as Darwin and Wallace had propounded the theory of the origin of species and natural selection; adding a sketch on sociobiology, with a word about the nature-nurture controversy.

Only George clapped at that, and Cohn could not figure out if he knew what he was doing or was he trying to crush an imaginary fly between his palms?

Cohn then noted man's ambivalent nature, the no-in-yes, evil-in-good, death-in-life, illusion-in-real, the complex, joyous-heartbreaking way it had worked out. Was the basic split caused by body-soul? Or was it God's withdrawal from His own presence? How would that go? Freud, an unbeliever, spoke of a secret trauma in His mind, converted to pain Everywhere.

"That brings us to evil—wherever it begins or how far goes: a metaphysical dripping, perhaps we can't account for, resulting in the appearance of Satan himself, whom I will discourse on for a couple of lectures at a later date—in particular, whether the Lord tore him out of His own mind and flung him into the bottomless pit out of which he afterwards crawled as a smoking snake; and has since then taken out on man his loss of angelic form and privilege—anyway, if Satan is allowed to go slithering around in Paradise, there's bound to be serious conflict and conflagration. In essence, the old boy envies man, wants to be him. Didn't he desire Eve when he saw her rolling bare-skinned in the flowers with Adam naked? 'Where's mine of that?' the old snake said when he met her in the wood; and she modestly responded, 'It isn't for you, for reasons I can't say.' He poisoned her apple after that. Broke her tree, it stopped singing hymns."

Cohn then sketchily recounted Freud's work and to prove it apt began summarizing certain aspects of human history, not excluding major wars fought and other useless disasters. "Man had innumerable chances but was—in the long run—insufficient to God's purpose. He was insufficient to himself. Some blame it on a poisoned consciousness, caused, for some chemical reason, by our lunatic genes running wild. More about that in the near future. Anyway, man doing a not-so-hot job, by and large, in his relations to other men—he loves only finger-deep. Love is not a popular phenomenon. Talks and talks but the real thing goes only finger-deep. Anyway, in all those ages he hardly masters his nature enough to stop the endless slaughter. What I mean," said Cohn, "is he never mastered his animal nature for the good of all—please excuse the word—I am an animal myself—nor could he invent a workable altruism. In short, he behaved too often irrationally, unreasonably, savagely, bestially. I'm talking, obviously, about constant overkill.

"And more of the same throughout human history. Please don't say I am hypersensitive—I'm talking at a time of almost total extinction, except us few. I will go into the Historical Past in six lectures I have planned; and the Twentieth Century Up to Now, in another two, the second beginning with the Holocaust that I mentioned yesterday: all that Jewish soap from those skeletal gassed bodies; and not long after that, since these experiences are bound to each other, the U.S. Americans drop the first atom bombs—teensy ones—on all those unsuspecting 8 a.m. Japanese crawling in broken glass to find their eyeballs. I could say more but haven't the heart."

Cohn said it wasn't his intention to exaggerate the extent of man's failures, willed or otherwise. Nor would he slight his capacity for good and beauty. "The reason I may seem to you to dwell heavily on the sins of man is to give you something to think about so you may, in a future chimpanzee society, avoid repeating man's worst errors. The future lies in your hands."

Ongoing heavy applause. Buz waved a green cap of Cohn's he had taken to wearing lately. Esau reluctantly pat-patted his moist palms. Mary Madelyn's eyes glowed tenderly, and Melchior, though he called it "pretty dry stuff," blew his nose and sentimentally frowned.

Cohn took a bow. Here's Calvin Cohn, one

man left on earth, teaching apes concerning man's failures. Not bad. His father the rabbi, may he rest in peace, would surely have approved.

(—Listen, Colvin, I never liked that you changed your name from Seymour to Colvin—a big naarishkeit—but what you say to the monkeys, this I like.

—Those aren't monkeys, Papa, those are full-grown primates.

—To me it's all the same, a monkey is a monkey.)

Cohn, unable to slow down his lecture, speculated that man failed because he was imperfect to begin with. "Never mind free will. How can we be free if the mind is limited by its constitution? Why hadn't the Almighty—in sum—done a better job? It wouldn't have been all that hard for Him—whether man appeared first as a gene with evolutionary potential, or as Adam himself and his rib fully formed—to have endowed him with a little more control over his instincts; and if not pure love for the human race, possibly for reasons of natural selection, then maybe at least enough feeling to be moved by their common plight—that many have little, and many have nothing—and that they are alive for a minute and die young?

"Am I wrong about that?"

Dead silence.

Melchior coughed.

"In other words," Cohn desperately ran on, "why should the Lord's imperfect creation have spoiled His originally extraordinary idea? Why hadn't He created man equal to whom He had imagined?"

Thus Cohn had aimed his arrow at God and was invisibly aimed at.

Buz afterward swore it was he who had first seen a Pillar of Fire descending the darkened sky.

(—At the very least you ought to have called it to my attention.

—I liked thot story you were telling us and wonted it to go on.)

The fearful apes sensed something about to happen and were afraid to move or they would have jumped screaming from the tree.

ALL ONE SAW WAS LIGHT.

""Why do you contend
with Me, Mr. Cohn?""

Cohn had shriveled, but wearing his father the cantor's white yarmulke kept him going. "I humbly ask to understand the Lord's intention."

""Who are you
to understand

the Lord's intention?
How can I explain
my mystery
to your mind?
Can a cripple ascend
a flaming of stars?""

"Abraham and Job contended," Cohn heard himself say.

""They were my servants.""

"Job complained You destroyed the blameless as well as the wicked."

""Job therefore repented.""

Cohn shook his enraged fist. "You have destroyed mankind. Our children are all dead. Where are justice and mercy?"

Holy Moses, he thought. Am I deranged? What am I doing to me?

Something knocked him with a bounce off his stool. He lay in a flopping heap on the earth.

""I am the Lord Thy God
who created man
to perfect Himself.""

* * *

The chimpanzees, crouching on high branches in the schooltree, watched, hushed, as Cohn lay writhing in dead leaves.

Mary Madelyn looked on with her eyes slammed shut. None dared approach Cohn. Nor would Buz move after the Pillar of Fire had ascended the heavens.

A wind wailed, pregnant with forked flashes and thunderous roars. The apes clung with hands and feet to the swaying, creaking, hissing eucalyptus. George the gorilla was seasick in his heaving cedar.

Cohn felt a trickle of bitter rain penetrate his lips and waked, groaning.

"Something hit me on the bone of my head."

He fell back on his stool, holding a book above him to keep the yellow raindrops from pounding his headache.

The drenched chimps held their places—barely—as the lashing wet wind diminished and the storm rose like a yellow balloon someone had let go.

Buz, from the top of the slippery tree, called the lecture a knockout. "When is the next episode?"

Cohn had no idea. His nose dripped ice water. He had caught a heavy cold and must go home. "I may have walking pneumonia. There won't be any school tomorrow."

Sincere, prolonged applause, drowning out

Esau's bray of contempt, rocked the schooltree.

And the ground was covered with lemons but no one had been hit except Cohn on his conk.

Melchior said, "My, all the lemonade we can shqueeze out of all those big lemonzh."

The Virgin in the Trees

Buz swore he had spied a black bottle in the frothy waves.

"Where in the frothy waves?"

"There in the ocean."

"Miserable child, why didn't you fish it out? You can swim."

"You said we had all the bottles we would ever need," Buz swore.

"That bottle had to be different," said Cohn.

"How would I know thot foct?"

As the sun broke through the morning mist three strangers appeared on the island beach a mile below Cohn's cave. Cohn studied them through his surveyor's glass, feeling uneasy. Where could they have come from? Is God replenishing the earth, or is the earth replenishing itself? The chimps sat in the sand diagonally opposite one another, touching toes. Buz hadn't slept in the cave that night. Cohn snatched up his full banana basket, plus a half-dozen coconut bars, and hurried to the beach.

By the time he arrived at the water all the other chimpanzees of the island community had assembled to greet the newcomers. Buz and Mary Madelyn, self-engrossed Esau, gentle Melchior, and the twins, were sniffing at or being sniffed by the new apes. They kissed, patted backs, grunted, embraced. None acted as a stranger, as if the world had shrunk too small for that. Cohn's companions had at first frightened the visitors by addressing them in human speech but then reverted to their primate language, which only the twins had partially forgotten.

"Do any of you know any of them?" Cohn, in a straw hat, standing barefoot in the hot sand with his banana basket, asked Buz.

"No," said Buz, "but we like them."

"Well done," said Cohn, "but who are they and where have they come from?"

"They say they don't know thot."

"Was it high ground or low?"

"They say it was either one or the other."

"Could they have got here by boat—maybe our old raft?—I mean from some other island?"

"They hov no boats or rofts. Their footsteps

come out of the woods, but not out of the water."

Buz said he would know more about the visitors after he had taught them to speak like the others.

Cohn said the sooner the better. "I am eager to know how they escaped the Second Flood." He cheerfully passed out some overripe bananas and candy bars to the three new chimps, who ate hungrily what he offered them. The two males, good-humored, one tall, the other stocky with bowed legs, had glossy brown coats. The old grandmother chimp sported ragged ears, teeth worn to the gums, and a threadbare behind.

Cohn, before Buz could make suggestions, called the old female Hattie, after an aunt; and the males he named Bromberg—the monkish tall one—and Esterhazy, the short other—after two college friends whose names he liked to be able to say once more.

Melchior enjoyed making the acquaintance of Hattie. He chucked her under the chin. They gamboled in the sand, huffing and panting, pushing each other down on their backs, tickling until they gasped.

Esterhazy, a bookkeeperish-looking ape, swallowed his soft banana without bothering to remove the peel; and Bromberg, a sweet-toothed type, applied himself to a coconut candy bar, teasing it with his tongue. When Saul of Tarsus and Luke begged for a piece, lifting their palms, he broke off two minute bites, handed one to each twin, and grunting, patted their heads. After wearing out the first candy bar he swallowed the second in a lip-sucking gulp.

Esau then informed the newly arrived brothers that he was the Alpha Ape of the island; and neither of them, although they seemed to consider the news seriously, objected.

The brothers watched Mary Madelyn in fascination, and sniffed at her rear, to her acute embarrassment, to determine whether she was in heat; apparently she wasn't. Mary Madelyn climbed a tree and sat in it, hidden by leafy branches.

In the afternoon, Bromberg and Esterhazy sat in a fig tree, plucking and eating ripe figs as they watched Cohn's community going through its varied chores—except for Esau, who was squatting on the ground poking long straws into the mound-nests of nonexistent ants.

And the next morning the newcomer apes sat hunched under the schooltree but refused to join the others in the branches, as if embarrassed by their lack of language, while Cohn discoursed on the first ice age. Those in the tree listened to the lecture in a mood resembling stupefied absorption. Saul of Tarsus broke into shivers, and Luke, after watching him a minute, joined him. Mary Madelyn sat hunched up in anticipation of Cohn's next freezing sentence. Melchior chewed thoughtfully on a leftover matzo from the seder, as he listened.

Buz dangled in suspense by one arm from an upper limb of the eucalyptus; and George the gorilla at length dropped out of his cedar to think something over; he headed, knucklewalking, into the rain forest, frightening Esterhazy, Bromberg, and Hattie, who hastily ascended the schooltree and at once became students. Sometime afterwards, during a whispered conversation with Buz, they began to speak in a human tongue.

These were productive days. Cohn had taken to throwing and baking clay pots; also to practicing herbal medicine, a development that brought the community closer together because they appreciated having an attending physician.

Always a collector, Cohn liked to take samples of grasses, herbs, leaves, and barks of various trees, some of which he boiled up in water and evaporated, to produce an extract of each substance. He sampled these concoctions, bitter and sweet, and found that one calmed his stomach if he had overeaten, and another lightened a severe headache.

Buz complained his eyes were strained and Cohn advised him to cut down on reading, but Buz wouldn't because he liked the stories he was becoming acquainted with. "Everything gets to be a story," he said, and Cohn agreed. He brewed up a mimosa ointment with boric acid, a concoction that reduced his boy's eyestrain.

For most minor ailments Cohn prescribed a mixture of eucalyptus oil and bicarbonate of soda. Either his patients vomited up the medication and improved in health, or kept it down and got better. With the same prescription he purged Saul of Tarsus, and Luke, of "worms," which couldn't really have been worms because they no longer lived on earth, though they resembled worms. Whatever they were, Cohn eradicated them. He also calmed Esau's toothache, offering to pull the offending molar with a pair of pliers, at which the Alpha Ape bristled threateningly and hooted sternly. He informed Cohn he no longer felt the toothache.

George the gorilla still loitered in the vicinity of Cohn's cave, usually when the cantor was singing, but he refused to enter and be treated for illness when he seemed to be ailing, though one day he suffered a severe, nose-dripping, eye-tearing, sneezy cold, for which Cohn wanted to prescribe an herb that would clear his breathing.

George refused to accept it.

"If you like to suffer," Cohn said to the gorilla, "that's your choice."

George sneezed seven times and Cohn uttered one "God bless."

Calvin Cohn had baked his early pots in midday sunlight but they hadn't turned out well. In his last large dig in the field beyond and above the rice paddy, he had discovered a muddy vein of white hydrous aluminum silicate clay, with which he began to mold unique dishes, bowls, vases, artificial flowers, other artifacts of decoration. He fired these in a kiln he had constructed in the fireplace, a simple metal "firebox" he had fabricated out of a ship's locker; this he heated with homemade charcoal of ebony wood that got so hot the box glowed vermilion and took hours to cool. Buz was uncomfortable in the presence of the red-hot kiln, yet as he lurked by the cave opening, he liked to watch Cohn remove the fired objects, some severely cracked because there was no temperature control.

Cohn, to the chimp's amusement, had lately begun to design clay masks sculpted with faces of Greek gods, former politicians, famous scientists of the past, some of whom he hung up as a mobile on a tree near the eucalyptus; and he created a few vertebrate animals the chimp had never laid eyes on. Cohn hadn't learned how to glaze his pots, so he painted the white clay masks with features colored in black, green, red, and yellow inks.

Buz saw his first lion's head as a mask produced by Cohn. Afterwards the artist destroyed many of the masks, fearing that the Lord, if He got a peek at them, might accuse him of worshipping false gods.

* * *

The island community was active and flourished beyond Cohn's best hopes. All the chimps, even the newcomers, were gainfully employed, with the exception of Esau, who lived on the fruit of the island. "Why disturb yourself if the fruit is for free? Why spoil our natures to please a non-chimp? Who is he, for instance?"

Cohn wouldn't say.

Saul of Tarsus and Luke helped in the rice paddy, Melchior overseeing them. Sometimes he fell asleep, standing, and the twins stopped working until he awoke and then asked for a banana-beer break, a custom Melchior favored.

Mary Madelyn assisted Cohn in collecting roots, leaves, new samples of bark. She watched him catalogue each item on a 3x5 card.

"I wish I had a handwriting, Cawvin."

"Maybe someday."

"Wiw I someday be human?"

"It's a long haul."

"I would wike to be Juwiet in wov with Romeo."

Cohn was growing a brown beard as he became bald.

Buz was, page by page, reading through the encyclopedia. His dod permitted him to use his personal reading eyeglasses, and they seemed to ease a slight strabismus.

Hattie had for a while looked after the twins, who resisted her motherly ministrations. She then took care of Melchior and he permitted her to build a sleep-nest near his in a low live oak.

Cohn stored away in dry caves full plastic bags of newly discovered sunflower seeds.

The chimps helped plant banana groves and other fruit trees. Esterhazy and Bromberg willingly assisted.

And everyone congregated around Buz and Cohn at their dig in the late afternoon. They sniffed and—to Cohn's annoyance—sometimes chewed on the ancient animal bones he had unearthed. To those who retched, he had to dispense gallons of eucalyptus-bicarb medicine for their dyspepsia.

He had occasional hopes that Buz might ask to be bar mitzvah'd since he was already the equivalent of age thirteen, but the little chimp never brought the matter up, and Cohn did not proselytize.

Life was serene until Mary Madelyn, the jeweled pink flower of her swollen sexual skin visible from the rear, hid herself from the pursuing males by taking to the tops of tall trees, but when the wind hit her dense scent—a compound of night-blooming jasmine and raw eggs, it seemed to Cohn—and blew it around, they went hungrily seeking and could not locate her although they ran through every tree in the vicinity.

Esau sought her relentlessly, sniffing his small-eyed way from branch to branch, breathing stertorously, restless with desire. Once after not finding her, he pounded in frustration on the trunk of the tree they had just explored.

Esterhazy and Bromberg, on the run, were ascending and descending one or another tree where they thought they had glimpsed the tempting flower, or caught an enticing trace of her sexual perfume. One dark day they pounced on someone who turned out to be Hattie, and happily crouched, but they seemed to have lost interest.

After catching an invigorating breath of Mary Madelyn's scent in the headlong breeze, Buz had decided he was mature enough to be interested and had joined the apes in pursuit of her; as had the twins because the chase was fun. They were caught up in adventure, spying out Mary Madelyn and swiftly shinnying up a tree to entrap her, but she escaped, and went squealing through the treetops. They pursued her until, by virtue of her inspired speed, she outdistanced them and disappeared in a curtain of green.

One still morning, Esau, bored with the school lesson, happened to spot her hiding in George the gorilla's cedar; she had been secretly listening to Cohn lecturing on the fossils of the Mesozoic age. Mary Madelyn had been thus engaged for three days, apparently with the connivance or unconcern of George, in an attempt to keep up with her lessons.

Esau, his head hair erect, stealthily climbed higher and higher in the eucalyptus and swung into the cedar on a vine. He descended in a leap and charged at Mary Madelyn as she sat absorbed in Cohn's description of a dinosaur attempting to defend itself in a bloody swamp against a rapacious flying reptile.

Catching sight of Esau, Mary Madelyn let out a full scream, interrupting Cohn's lecture, and at once leaped to the ground, the males in hot pursuit. George the gorilla roared at the contretemps, and the noise seemed to paralyze the other apes in the schooltree, although it had no effect, to speak of, on Esau. Cohn bellowed at him to leave the girl alone.

The uncooperative chimp, chasing her on the ground, caught Mary Madelyn by the arm and hurled her against a tree. She went down with the breath knocked out of her, bleeding from a wound over her left eye. Before Esau, swaggering from foot to foot, could compel her to crouch, she tore herself out of his grasp and swung into a vast baobab, immediately losing herself in it. In a minute she was brachiating like a gibbon through the rain forest, zig-zagging in the foliage as Esau furiously hooted after her.

Gaining on her, he was a moment from overtaking Mary Madelyn, when she reversed direction and dipped under him. He grabbed for her where she no longer was, and fell halfway through a tree. Esau hit the ground hard and lay motionless on his back.

Mary Madelyn had disappeared.

Bromberg and Esterhazy had abandoned the contest between the dinosaur and pterodactyl to see what was going on in the modern world. They stopped off to prop Esau up, who would have none of it. He rose on his knees and stomped the earth in rage.

Cohn, after his interrupted lecture, confided to Buz that Esau had become a hazard to a free society and must reform, or they might have to consider getting rid of him.

"Why don't we get rid of her?"

"I thought you were interested in Mary Madelyn?"

"Not when she runs whenever she sees me. It says in Dr. Bünder's book that female chimponzees seek male compony when they go into heat. Why doesn't she do whot the book says?"

Cohn thought she seemed to be resisting her instincts.

Buz asked why.

He wasn't sure. "Something in her. She's an unusual person—which is to say, chimpanzee."

Buz thought she was mad. "How om I supposed to experience sex if she won't stond still for holf a minute?"

Cohn suggested he seek out and persuade

her. "My sense of it is she would like to be courted, not gunned down from the rear by an ambitious phallus. Talk to her about *Romeo and Juliet.* She admires the play."

Buz said he disliked it. "They are both goons and so is Mary Modelyn."

"She's a sensitive, empathic, intelligent creature."

That night he was awakened by the rustling of his ivy curtain. Cohn struck a match and held the flickering flame above his head.

"Who's there?"

Mary Madelyn squatted amid the shadows on the floor of the cave.

"I have no safe pwace to go. May I pwease stay the night?"

"Why don't you make yourself a nest in a tree? The males should be sleeping now."

"No, they aren't." She was fatigued, forlorn, disquieted.

"Turn your head till I get my pants on," Cohn told her.

When he had drawn them on he said she could stay, and lit the lamp.

She wanted to rest on some branches on the cave floor, but he said she could have Buz's cage. "He almost never uses it."

Mary Madelyn promised to leave before the sun was up.

He offered her a drink of coconut juice. As he poured, Cohn observed her flabby, wilted flower, and the sight of it made him slightly ill.

"It wiw go away soon," she said apologetically.

"I can't understand why you resist every male who approaches you."

She said it was in part his fault. "You wanted us to wearn your wanguage. Now that I have, I am different than I used to be. If I hadn't wearned to speak and understand human speech, I would have awready presented mysewf to every mawe on the iwand."

She asked Cohn if he would mate with her.

"It is not permitted. I am a man. I am not allowed to copulate with animals."

"You told us you were proud to be an animal."

"Of course. Generically speaking."

"You would be mistaken to think of me only as a beast," Mary Madelyn said.

She said she had decided to sleep elsewhere.

Hairy Esau, lugging a knobby log four feet long and three inches thick, lurched into Cohn's cave the next morning. "Where's the bitch hiding?"

He let out a roar, his yellowed fangs repulsively visible, and raised the log as though to bash Cohn's mind in.

He rose hastily from his unfinished breakfast. "You're mistaken, she's not here."

"Saul of Tarsus saw her sneak in last night."

Cohn swore she had left. His scalp stung as if his hair had turned into needles. How does one reason with a mad chimp who confuses himself with a gorilla? Fearing for his life, Cohn had backed toward the storage shelves—the breakfast table the only barrier between him and the grossly angered ape.

"Don't be overhasty, Esau. This is a desperately serious situation. The world has been destroyed by fire and water. You heard my recent lecture on the subject. I have reason to believe that those of us left on this island are the only survivors of life on the planet. If we expect to go on living we've got to live as brothers. Why don't you put that nasty log down and let's discuss the matter peaceably."

Esau, breathing noisily, his small eyes restlessly roaming the cave, called Cohn an idiot. "Your stupid schooltree has made her too proud to dip her butt for friends."

He swung his log at Cohn, who ducked, barely escaping having his head crushed. Stealthily he felt behind him for his 30.06 Winchester, at the same panicky instant thinking, I mustn't use it.

If he could tease the French saber out of its sheath, the sight of it might scare the beast away. Esau kept his brutal log raised as he inched toward Cohn, who was then assailed by a more frightening thought: Is he the Lord's messenger who has this day come to slay me?

Without waiting for a formal response, he overturned the table between them. Esau was scalded by a pot of hot mint tea.

The ape let out a quavering cry that rose to a scream when he dropped the log on his burnt foot. His mouth dribbled and eyes bled tears of rage.

Cohn, instead of taking up a weapon, grabbed a witch's mask from the shelf and held it over his face, at the same time ululating and grunting.

It was a contorted white mask with watery red eyes, a nose like a bent bone, and wet black mouth. The mouth moved obscenely as Cohn howled.

Esau, erect in fright, stared wide-eyed at Cohn's horrid mask. He let out a whine, as if he had lost control of his bodily functions. Bolting out of the cave, he ran groaning into the forest. No one saw him for months afterwards.

After two days, Mary Madelyn, looking her neat, attractive self, returned to the schooltree to resume her education.

None of the male apes approached, or even seemed to notice her presence, but Cohn, on greeting her, had kissed her fingertips.

He thought he had handled Esau badly and would have to do better in the future, assuming the chimp returned. Esau must be patiently talked to and counseled until he understood what was required of him for the common good.

Cohn sent Buz into the forest to locate the rebellious Alpha Ape and ask him to return to the community, but Buz, after a full day's search, saw no sign of him and figured he had made for the headlands.

He told Cohn, in unconcealed trepidation, that an albino ape seemed to be in the woodland trees again.

"I saw him but he didn't see me."

"Who is this type and is he for real?" Cohn wanted to know.

"A white ape, they can be nasty people."

"Have you ever known one?"

"Dr. Bünder had a long porograph on them in his book. Sometimes they get schizoid, or like thot."

"He'd better stay out of here."

But on the next dark night the albino, grown a few feet since Cohn had last laid eyes on him, appeared in his cave. Either dawn broke then, or he lit the cave with his white presence.

Cohn hastily retreated to the rear.

Rising on his legs, the albino pantomimed flinging a spear at Cohn, or someone like him.

"That was like in a dream," Cohn explained. "I was attempting to defend myself, not hurt anybody."

To get rid of the ape, he reached for a black witch's mask hanging on a peg on the wall.

The ape tore the mask from Cohn's hand and held it in front of his face, becoming a white ape with a black face, pierced by a red witch's eye. The sight sent a chill through Cohn and he bolted the cave.

In the forest, in an instant, he encountered a black-faced white ape. Cohn squared off in the circling crouch of a grunting Japanese wrestler, to hold the ape off as best he could; but the fierce creature grabbed his arm and yanked him over his shoulder, his large paw grasping both of Cohn's hands, his long ape-arm pinning his kicking legs.

"Let's talk about this," begged Cohn.

The white ape, bumpily running with a struggling Cohn on his shoulders, leaped for a low bough of an ebony tree, and with his free hand, both legs, and a grunt, swung himself and his victim into the tree.

He'll destroy me up there. Should I try prayer, or is the white ape God's messenger come to execute His purpose?

"Are you God's messenger?"

If the ape knew he wouldn't say. He had with a vibrant roar stopped in his tracks.

Above them, holding to an upper branch, stood George the gorilla, his right hand aiming a large black coconut—if not a rock—at the head of the white ape carrying Cohn.

The tree began to shake as if it had conceived a mad thought, but the swaying gorilla held tight to his black object.

The ape released his hold on him and Cohn, freed, felt himself falling through the thick-leaved swaying ebony, bumping his head till it sickened him. He landed, with a swooshing thud, in a bouquet of giant ferns at the foot of the tree.

In the bright sunlight that broke through the forest canopy, the white ape seemed to dissolve, and the ebony stopped its frightful shaking. The forest was hushed.

Buz appeared in the undergrowth wearing a Japanese general's cap and blasting a long tin horn.

The nervous gorilla high in the tree thrust two fingers into each ear as Cohn tried to shake himself awake; but how could you if you hadn't slept?

A disturbing desire possessed him, fortunately yielding affection, not so easy to come upon these days. And affection grew against his will—a difficult way to love.

After the schooltree class they strolled amid the dappled palm trees lining the sea. Cohn walked at ease, Mary Madelyn standing upright or knuckle-walking by his side. When they rested she groomed his balding head. In turn, he groomed her breasts and belly. They talked as friends.

And Buz, forgetting his manners, persistently trailed them, and neither of them could convince him to leave them to their privacy. He hung around, eavesdropping, hiding behind the trunks of trees, or pretending to be asleep as they sat on the ground. Sometimes he brachiated quietly above them, observing their actions. Cohn, when he spotted him, recalled the serpent licentiously regarding Adam and Eve in intercourse.

They liked holding hands as they walked together. Mary Madelyn, after consuming a passion fruit he had picked for her, kissed Cohn full on the lips.

Buz complained high in a tree. He shredded bark with his teeth, obviously deeply jealous.

He had told Cohn he was old enough for sexual experience and wished to copulate with Mary Madelyn. He didn't know by what right his own dod interfered with his courtship of her. She was his kind, not Cohn's.

Cohn said that on this island there was only one kind—sentient, intelligent living beings. "We're sort of affectionately in love," he told Buz, "or something close to it."

Buz wanted to be in love too, and Cohn replied his time would come. He mentioned Hattie, and Buz hooted in ridicule. The chimp stomped away but got over being angry with Cohn in less than a week. Instead of following the lovers, he began to collect rare stones and shells on the beach. Cohn had taught the rudiments of polishing stones, and had also told him some appealing stories of sublimation. Buz said he didn't like the stories, yet it was apparent he had learned something. On the other hand, he formally moved out of the cave, taking along eight cream coconut bars and an old hat of Cohn's.

Cohn agreed it was time Buz had a place of his own, though he expected him to drop in at the cave whenever he felt like it. If he happened to be busy, he was sure Buz would understand.

On their wandering walks, or as they rested in the warm grass, or sat together in a tree, Mary Madelyn and he talked about *Romeo and Juliet.* Cohn had read her the first act three times, and she greatly enjoyed the balcony scene. She liked to say, "'What wov can do, that dares wov attempt.'"

She had never seen a balcony and imagined a vine-entangled baobab in which Juliet was confined by two hefty, threatening guardian apes. Then Romeo, a youthful, handsome chimpanzee, appeared, scared off the offensive apes with a display of strength, and released Juliet from her prison-tree. They lived together, afterwards, in his happy flowering acacia.

Cohn didn't tell her about the sad future fate of the lovers. He would let her find that out herself. Mary Madelyn was not the curious reader Buz was, yet she liked to be read to and learned well by ear.

"Am I wovwy as Juwiet?" she asked Cohn.

"You have your graces."

"Wiw you ever wov me?"

He couldn't say yes nor did he say no. Cohn said love was complicated but they were obviously affectionate to each other.

"What is wov?" Mary Madelyn asked.

Cohn said it was a flame that lights a flame. "That's how a romantic would put it." He was eager to educate her.

Mary Madelyn, listening dreamily, wanted to know what other kind of love there was.

"A living-together kind of love, however romantically it may have begun, something trusting, sustaining, committed to life."

"Can I wov wike that?"

"I hope so."

"If I do, wiw you wov me?"

He said he thought so.

"I wov you," she said to Calvin Cohn.

He said he found her engaging. She was even alluring these days, amiable brown eyes, silken black hair; her features approached human. Though Mary Madelyn could not be said to be classically beautiful—facts were facts—still beauty existed, derived to some degree from her intelligent, generous nature. She came to something. Having become aware of her quality, her spirit, Cohn thought, accounted for his growing feeling for her.

Sensing receptivity, Mary Madelyn presented herself to him, crouching low. Her sexual skin, after four weeks, had blossomed overnight, like a repellent flower.

Cohn said he was sorry but he couldn't possibly oblige—couldn't mount her.

"Why not? You said you fewt affection for me."

He admitted he did but could only embrace her face to face. "I wouldn't be surprised if love began that way—evolutionarily speaking," he said, "when two lovers were able to face one another."

She said she was perfectly willing to embrace him face to face, and afterwards they could mate as nature demanded.

Cohn then said the act was forbidden to him—"to copulate with an animal."

"Is that *aw* I am to you?"

"Certainly not. But I have to take other things into account. My father was a religious man. I've been influenced by his teaching, not to mention his moral vision, and also his temperament." Cohn said that as a young man he had broken from his father and gone his own way, but he was still bound to him, although he had been dead for years and Cohn's own world had been destroyed.

Mary Madelyn, getting back to the practical, said she had taken a bath that morning. She told him she was pure. "I have kept my virginity for you ever since you expwained the world to me when you first read me *Romeo and Juwiet.*"

He now understood her frantic flights from the male apes, and admired her for saving herself for him on his terms, an astonishing feat for an animal, even a primate.

Yet he replied, "It says in Leviticus, 'Thou shalt not let thy cattle gender with a diverse kind—'"

"I am not a cattew."

"It also says, 'If a man lies with a beast he shall be put to death; and you shall kill the beast.' And it says more or less the same in Deuteronomy: 'Cursed be he who lies with any kind of beast.'"

"Do you think of me as a beast, Cawvin?"

"Not really," he admitted.

Mary Madelyn asked him if he had a mind of his own; and the next moment she was in flight, having spied a band of males in a nearby tree—Buz among them—who had beheld, and were discussing, her shivering pale flower.

Cohn, shouting and waving his arms, diverted them as Mary Madelyn took off for, and escaped, into the rain forest.

How can I love her? he reflected in his cave, except as I loved my dog?

During the tropical night a haggard Mary Madelyn appeared in the cave, and when Cohn sleepily lit the lamp, she presented herself to him.

He blew out the light and turned toward the wall.

She slept in Buz's cage and in the morning

swept the floor with a bramble broom and was gone.

She did not appear in the schooltree, and neither did the young males. Only Melchior and Hattie attended class that day, squatting on a branch of the eucalyptus, holding hands.

And George, in his coniferous cedar, sat alone as usual, cracking palm nuts with his rock-like teeth as he listened, the short hair on his sloping dark skull rising as Cohn lectured on the development of the great apes and ascent of homo sapiens during the course of evolution. He had several times lectured on natural selection—the maximization of fitness, someone had defined it—a popular subject with his students. It promised possibilities if one made himself—or in some way became—selectable.

And the chimpanzees liked to learn where they might have originated. They enjoyed the mysteries of being and becoming, of guessing and knowing. Cohn used some of the fossils he had dug out of the earth to illustrate and trace the anatomical development of mammals. He said he had had great hopes for the future of man, until the Day of Devastation. Cohn had at one time theorized that evolution might produce a moral explosion via a gifted creature, homo ethicalis; but man, as he was, had got there first with a different kind of explosion.

In class the next morning, after a night of sleeping thinking of Mary Madelyn, he was not as carefully prepared as usual, yet he addressed himself to the subject of the close relationship of chimpanzees and the creature who had once lived on earth as man, a closer relationship than Darwin might have imagined. They were descended from a common ancestor, perhaps Ramapithecus, who lived about twenty million years ago, a gifted apelike primate who may have been struck—it seemed to Cohn—by a crafty desire to improve his lot in life, if not altogether to change himself into something better than he assumed he was.

"The physical similarities of chimpanzee and man show in their blood and brain," Cohn lectured, "as well as in their appearance and behavior. Human beings—this will interest you—and great apes have almost identical genes—more than 99 percent of the amino-acid sequences in human beings and African apes are identical, despite morphological differences. And the African apes' albumin antibody reactions are (let's say) closer to men's than they were (let's say) to Asian apes. All this indicates about five million years since we diverged from a common ancestor on the molecular clock, which is very impressive, I'd say."

Cohn cited Dr. Walther Bünder as his source, and the two old chimps in the tree clapped heartily. The gorilla, still cracking palm nuts with his teeth, listened raptly, sometimes forgetting to chew.

Cohn went on: "Also in their sensory apparatus, the nature of their emotions, and their expressions and grimaces—perhaps even in who they think they are, chimpanzees are more like men than some men, or any other primate.

"Though they can be as nasty, brutish, and mean as men, their natures are essentially affectionate. They kiss and hug on celebratory occasions, and some—I have heard—even die of broken hearts."

Here Hattie dabbed her eye with eucalyptus leaves, and Melchior sniffed once.

But George the gorilla gave his chest a muffled thump, as if in doubt he was hearing good news; and sighed to himself.

"The idea I wish to propound," Cohn suggested, "is that it seems entirely possible that chimpanzees, as they progress in their evolution may, if their unconscious minds insist, incite molecular changes that will sooner or later—sooner, I hope—cause them to develop into a species something like man, perhaps better than man was when he fell from grace and vanished"—Cohn coughed to dislodge a frog in his throat—"from the face of this earth.

"And if these forthcoming chimps do, in the long run, turn out to be more fortunate than man—maybe a little more richly endowed, more carefully controlled, more easily inclined to the moral life; in the larger sense more "humanly" behaved than the species of which I am the last survivor; then maybe the presently disaffected Almighty Being Who began the creation of us all may bestow on them a more magnanimous fate than homo sapiens achieved—I mean suffered."

Cohn personally felt that the Lord, when He saw such good-willed alteration going on among the chimps who had selected themselves, might once more love His creation.

"God's there, sure enough," he said, "sitting in his judgment seat, but not always attentive to what's going on, as if He has on His mind one of His new concerns—in this case a gob of bacteria He had that day laid under a warm rock on Pluto; and as a result he suffers a cosmic absentmindedness caused by being conscious of *everything* at every instant of existence, or duration, or whatever it is that, among infinite other qualities, we call God's Being—That-Which-Is-Above-Is-Below-and-What-Is-Inside-Is-Outside-Kind-of-Being. Yet surely He will welcome, when He notices, a species of adventurous chimps developing into a species of superior-sort-of-men?

"Amen," Cohn muttered.

Melchior and Hattie, at the conclusion of this inspired address, applauded enthusiastically, and quickly descended the schooltree for their banana beer.

George dropped out of his cedar like a long lump of putty, as if dismayed he hadn't heard a gorilla mentioned once, and he loped away.

Cohn then reconsidered a daring plan that had filtered through his thoughts last night as Mary Madelyn slept in his cave. In the morning he plotted it on a sheet of paper he afterwards destroyed.

He had decided that the extraordinary act he had in mind might be worth a stab in the dark. Doubts assailed him—contemplating a fantastic act of daring was like a trumpet blast, the soldiers of doubt woke and charged—but Cohn cleverly sidestepped them.

If he and Mary Madelyn, in mutual affection, lay with each other, and however he aimed and entered, he succeeded in depositing in her hospitable uterus a spurt of adventurous sperm: *that*—if it took—might sooner or later have the effect he was hoping for. Assuming fertilization, and carrying her fetus to full term (the odds against that, he had learned from Dr. Bünder, were high), she would, with luck, give birth to a baby in eight months. Whatever happened thereafter was uncertain, but the beginning—without which nothing began but God Himself—would have begun.

In sum, a worthy primate evolution demanded, besides a few macroevolutionary lucky breaks, a basis of brainpower; and commencing with a combination of man-chimp child, the two most intelligent of God's creatures might produce this new species—

ultimately of Cohn's invention—an eon or two ahead on the molecular clock.

Let's see what happens now.

Cohn reasoned thus: Already his citizen-chimps had mastered language as speech and foundation of rational thought. Assuming the presence, not too long from now (Look how quickly Adam and Eve, a single couple who did not work hard at it, had peopled the earth), of the necessary females, and as a result of Cohn's "experiment" a rich pool of genes to work with—sooner or later the developing man-apes would inherit larger, more complex, more subtle brains than either now possessed; and who knows what other useful characteristics, also freely bestowed, might be achieved in comparatively less future-time, evolutionarily speaking, if God did not interfere with (indeed, secretly sanctioned and blessed) the process.

Who knows—Cohn let it play in his mind—maybe the Lord had reconsidered His Second Dismal Flood and was regretting it. He Himself, possibly, had inspired the revolutionary impulse in Cohn's head—(His vessel)—that he mate with a lady ape; despite which act He would omit cursing him, and thereafter killing the innocent "beast," such primeval punishment null and void in these ineluctably post-Torah times?

And wouldn't Cohn be playing a role in

purpose like that of Lot's daughters, who lay down with their wine-drunk father after Sodom had been smoked off the map, to preserve the future of mankind and its successors, not excluding the Messiah?

If two daughters, in a dark cave on separate nights, lay incestuously with their wine-sotted, love-groaning father, why not Cohn, a clearheaded, honest man, lying with biophilial affection and shut eyes, against the warm furry back of a loving lady chimpanzee who spoke English well and was mysteriously moved by *Romeo and Juliet?*

He considered renaming the island, "Cohn's Lot."

But his doubts were these: he had recalled the fable of the cat changed into a princess, who as pretty princess—to the prince her husband's astonishment—pounced on a befuddled gray mouse who had blundered into the parlor. The next day the cat was back in the cat life.

What's bred in the bones lives there. Similarly, with or without speech, Mary Madelyn had armies of ancient chimpgenes tucked away in her flesh, that might overwhelm Cohn's civilized genotypes trying to make a living in her warm ape-womb. If they perished in the struggle to survive in a semi-alien fetus, how could Cohn contribute anything of lasting value to the child?

Or suppose the child was born a monster and for some inevitable genetic reason developed as King Kong, unless the old monster appeared on the scene as Queen?

Fooling around with evolution—for wasn't that what it ultimately came to?—despite good intentions, was a mad act for a hitherto responsible scientist. Besides, the future was beyond invisible reach, and he would never know what he had stirred up.

On the other hand, with so many doubts and maybes staring him in the face on this broken island, yet with fantastic possibilities on the horizon, or boiling up in the surrounding seas—maybe about to fly at him from another planet—so much one could not begin to foretell—therefore what else to do when there were no practical prospects at hand but "take a chance"? Some good might come of it. What worked, worked; what hadn't, might.

Therefore monkey with evolution? That much chutzpah?

Why not—in these times—if one took into account the eschatological living trauma the Lord had laid on the world?

That decided the matter for Cohn.

After the day's work, he unfolded the portion of stiff sail of the *Rebekah Q* that he had used as a seder tablecloth. Guiding a pair of tinsmith's shears along a charcoal line he had drawn to outline a simple dress pattern he had found in his one-volume, all-purpose, popular encyclopedia, Cohn cut out a portion of the canvas material into front and back panels of a simple chemise.

With a waxed twine inserted through an eye he had punched into a nail, he sewed together the two halves of the dress; and Cohn considered adding a pair of white drawers, but gave that up when it occurred to him they would only get in the way. When Mary Madelyn, groggy from outrunning pursuing males all day, returned to the cave, Cohn presented the white garment to her as a friendship gift.

She asked what she could do with it, and Cohn said he would like her to dress in it, and he would help if she needed help. Apparently she didn't. She went through the motions of clothing herself and seemed to enjoy dressing, though she swore she had never before in her life worn any garment except a hat of flowers she had once made for herself.

Cohn, stepping back to admire her elegant appearance in the white dress, said she looked like somebody's bride.

"Do I wook wike Juwiet?"

"Sort of, though I'm no Romeo."

"I wov you, do you wov me?"

"Sure enough," said Cohn. "I sure do."

Perhaps her eyes misted, perhaps not, but it seemed to Cohn that she would have cried a little if chimps could. Maybe someday—another step in their humanization.

Turning the lamp low, he proposed that she and he mate, and Mary Madelyn modestly assented.

He lifted her white skirt from the rear, and with shut eyes, telling himself to keep his thoughts level, Cohn dipped his phallus into her hot flower. There was an instant electric connection and Cohn parted with his seed as she possessed it. He felt himself happily drawn clean of sperm. Mary Madelyn was at once calmed. She waited a minute for more to happen, but when nothing more did, she chewed up a fig and fell asleep in his bed.

He lifted down from the top storage shelf the clay urn containing his former wife's ashes, and with his shovel buried it under a palm tree. Buz, in the night-dark, dug it up with his hands and flung the urn into the dimly moonlit sea.

Esau appeared, ghastly, one morning as Cohn was breakfasting in the cave. He rose, wildly seeking a weapon to defend his life with, then realized the dispirited ape was not well. He had lost about twenty pounds, his shaggy coat was soiled, and his left jaw swollen. His eyes were ten degrees crossed and bleary.

Esau said he suffered from a mind-blowing toothache; the pain tore his face apart. He begged Cohn to help him or he would go mad.

Cohn, after slipping on his glasses, administered an herb that put the chimp to sleep, and assisted by Mary Madelyn, pulled out the offending molar with a strong pair of pliers.

Esau, when he woke, was overjoyed the pain had ceased and expressed everlasting gratitude to Cohn. He promised to reform, and volunteered to assist the common effort. And to prove his resolve, he asked to be given a productive task to perform.

Cohn appointed him keeper of the orchard. It was his duty to report those trees that were flowering and about to come to fruit; also to look for fruit trees that hadn't been catalogued.

After the episode with Esau, Cohn wrote down seven Commandments he had been carrying in his head, and tried to think of a way of presenting them to the assembly of apes. He wasn't attempting to rewrite the Pentateuch, he told himself (and God); he was simply restating, or amplifying, some principles he had been reflecting on.

There was no nearby mountain from whose heights to come trudging down bearing two tablets in his arms, so Cohn baked each letter in white clay, assembled them into sentences, and set each up with twine, pegs, nails, and Elmer's glue, on the eastern face of the escarpment near the waterfall, where all who passed by on their way to the rice paddy, or big dig, would see them.

Cohn's Admonitions—he had decided to drop Commandments—read thus:

1. We have survived the end of the world; therefore cherish life. Thou shalt not kill.

2. Note: God is not love, God is God. Remember Him.

3. Love thy neighbor. If you can't love, serve—others, the community. Remember the willing obligation.

4. Lives as lives are equal in value but not ideas. Attend the Schooltree.

5. Blessed are those who divide the fruit equally.

6. Altruism is possible, if not probable. Keep trying. See 3 above.

7. Aspiration may improve natural selection. Chimpanzees may someday be better living beings than men were. There's no hurry but keep it in mind.

On the day the Admonitions were fixed on the wall of the escarpment, Cohn read them aloud to the assembled apes and led a cheer for each. The response to the 7th was moderate but he did not insist on another cheer.

* * *

The island colony prospered. All chimps worked, in fields and trees and in caves, collecting and storing food, seeding and caring for gardens, and distributing flowers to those who wanted to adorn their sleep-nests.

The rice paddies were extended, the twins doing much of the planting and harvesting. Melchior directed and Hattie helped. Not all members of the community cared for rice—Buz called it tasteless stuff, though Melchior said it was good to rub on aching gums—but Cohn kept hundreds of sacks stored in nearby caves in case of famine. He was not fearful of famine—hadn't dreamed of it in his dreams—was just being careful.

The schooltree was well attended every day. Esau, his sour face sweetened, sat on a branch close to Mary Madelyn, but did not trouble her. Buz sat on an upper bough, as far from her as he could arrange. On his own, he spent days working out arithmetic puzzles. He had asked Cohn to teach him algebra so he could go on sublimating.

Everyone enjoyed the pleasant weather—cool mornings, hot afternoons, chilly nights; and the chimps—all but the twins—tended to walk upright. George did not change; he was still the old knuckle-walking George, rather than flirt with backaches got from holding his 500-pound body erect. Buz, after chancing on the word in the dictionary, called him pariah; but the gorilla, though he might have crushed the little chimp's skull in his hands, paid him no attention. He kept his dignity.

On the important holidays Cohn played his father's records on the machine, and the apes danced a square dance in the green grass. Holidays came often that year, whenever anyone thought there ought to be one.

They called themselves "men." Esterhazy hooted, "Come on, men, let's get cracking." Cohn felt that evolution was peeking through them. He encouraged being healthy because it felt good, and for purposes of natural selection. He was voted teacher-for-life and honorary chimpanzee.

Mary Madelyn had taught herself to say lwov for wov, and was in her second month of pregnancy.

What was God doing in her womb?

The Voice of the Prophet

Eight baboons sat like black dogs in a circle on a large, flat, sandstone rock. One male bled from his left eye. The other had lost part of his snout and all but one right toe. If a leaf moved they screamed in alarm, their muzzles showing long mouthfuls of pointed teeth.

Each of the three females mothered one undernourished child. When the males threat-yawned, or snarled at each other, the females rose and paced tensely and gracefully on the rock, their children riding their backs, until the males had calmed down.

On the ground they ate tubers and fruit, and tore at dry grasses. They lapped water at the pond, often raising their heads to stare at the chimps tending the rice. When a baboon male barked in alarm the small troop galloped back to the rock, the females gracefully ascending its ledges, their children clinging to their backs.

Saul of Tarsus had spied the baboons from the rice field, and word by slow word, informed anyone who would listen that he had seen some strange black monkeys around. Melchior said they looked to him like baboons who had lived in a pit or dirty cave. He said they all needed baths. He personally had no use for any of them, and Hattie agreed.

At dusk the baboons were afraid of the dark. They leaped from the rock and fled across the grass to an old madrone where they built their sleep-nests. When night came they were asleep. Awaking, they seemed to fear each other until one day, after a dry season, the drenching rain washed the black out of their patchy coats, and turned them a greenish-yellow. After the rain they sat placidly on the rock, or galloped in the grass, back-flipping, tail-pulling, wrestling. The black stain—dye, mud, or ashes—washed out of their coats in the rain, had discolored the pond by the rice, and Melchior complained bitterly to Cohn, who thus learned of the presence of the baboons. For days he pondered God's purpose.

Mary Madelyn, after a time of doubt, when she bled and it seemed she might momentarily lose her fetus, having become securely pregnant, had one day disappeared from her favorite white acacia. Cohn had searched for her among the fruit trees in the woods, in the rain forest, and in caves in the escarpment, but could not, after several days, locate her.

He asked Hattie to help him find her and if necessary to stay with her while she gave birth, but Hattie said no chimpanzee lady in her right mind would need a midwife.

The next night Mary Madelyn appeared in Cohn's cave, trailing a bloody umbilical cord, and carrying a newborn baby she timidly presented to him.

Seeing a fuzzy white baby with human eyes, Cohn ran out of the cave because he thought he had affronted God; then he ran back because he felt he hadn't.

This was a different world from the one he had been born into. In a different world different things—unusual combinations—occurred. If something wasn't kosher the Lord would have to say so. He had no trouble with words.

The Lord said nothing.

With a pair of small sterilized scissors Cohn snpped Mary Madelyn's umbilical cord, washed and knotted it, then examined the new baby. She was a compact, well-formed, curious-eyed little female who looked, indeed, like a humanoid infant, or chimpanzee-human baby. She wasn't as large as an infant chimp, according to the measurements cited by Dr. Bünder in his book, but she was healthy, spirited, and obviously bright. Cohn counted aloud to ten, and she responded by moving her lips. He was sure she would do well in school.

"Do you wike her?"

"A miracle," said Cohn. "Why wouldn't I like her?"

"I wondered if you wanted a mawe chiwd."

He said the community needed all the females it could get.

Mary Madelyn said it wasn't that easy—chimpanzee ladies bore children only every four or five years.

Cohn said they would solve it one way or another. The birth of the baby made him feel more optimistic than he had been since arriving on the island.

The baby, as she nursed at her mother's breast, regarded him with bright eyes, human eyes. Cohn was thinking of his role in raising the child. With a chimpanzee mother she is technically a chimp, but I will keep reminding her of her human source and quality. A lot depends on which genes have gone where. If the right genes have arranged themselves to their best advantage, she'll be talking soon. In a month or two he would begin reading to her.

"Shaw we caw her Juwiet?"

Cohn suggested maybe Islanda, but when Mary Madelyn pronounced it Iwanda, he said Rebekah might be preferable.

Mary Madelyn liked Honeybunch, a name Cohn occasionally called her, but they settled, at his suggestion, on Rebekah Islanda as her legal first and middle names.

Yet when they talked to her, Mary Madelyn called her Iwanda and Cohn said Rebekah. He then asked Mary Madelyn if she would mind being called another name, maybe Rachel, but she preferred to keep her own name.

That night, Cohn, making a determined effort, finished nailing together the wall of split logs he had begun to assemble when the first new chimps had appeared on the island.

He mounted the wall on rollers he had constructed—slow, squeaky, but workable. To block the entrance, he had to shove with his shoulder to roll the creaking wall across the mouth of the cave. He had dug a narrow trench for the barrier to fit in, making it less likely to topple over if it ever was rammed from the outside. A chimp or two confronting it would have to give up and walk away. It wasn't the most practical bulwark he had ever seen, but Cohn felt it would serve its purpose.

Mary Madelyn wanted to know why they had to have a wall—it would keep the fresh air out that the baby needed; and Cohn replied he was just being careful. Civilization had barely recommenced.

When the chimps arrived in a group to see the new baby, Cohn permitted them all to enter, and served them a mixture of tangerine and mango juice, which they all enjoyed, no one seemed to notice the wall he had built.

Hattie picked up the baby, and Mary Madelyn permitted only her to do so. Melchior was allowed to pat Rebekah on the head; and Esau, to show his love of children, felt her bottom and then covered the child with her blanket, aware of Mary Madelyn's nervousness.

"Trust me," the Alpha Ape assured her. "I am her good fairy."

Buz, on the other hand, showed only a negative interest in the baby girl, insisting on dragging his holding cage out of the cave because he didn't want it to be used as a crib.

"What will you use it for?" Cohn asked.

Buz said, "Storage."

"Why don't you at least say hello to your little sister?"

Buz replied he had never had a relative other than the mother who had given birth to him, and his adoptive father, who had brought him up and educated him in his home in Jersey City, Dr. Walther Bünder, Ph.D., M.D.—the kindest, wisest, most loving person he had ever met in all his life.

Cohn felt unwillingly left out—omitted, deeply disappointed.

"Don't think I've lost my affection or admiration for you, Buz, I haven't."

Buz did say he would be returning for a candy bar now and then, but he seemed still angered, and Cohn felt he must give him more attention one way or another.

When the visiting chimps had left the cave, Mary Madelyn said she hoped their own little family would stay together, and Cohn said they would indeed while Rebekah was growing up.

"She may someday be the mother of a new race of men," he said, "—if they are called that then and not by some other name."

Mary Madelyn wondered if they ought to get married. "I wov the scene that you read me wast week where Romeo and Juwiet are married by Father Wawrence."

Cohn said for his father's sake he would prefer a sort of Jewish wedding.

The baboon males on the rock groomed each other, and the three females groomed themselves and their children. Cohn had named the little girl Sara, and the boys Pat and Aloysius, after two Irish public-school chums of many years ago. Sometimes the children groomed the adult males.

One early afternoon Sara descended the rock with an unpeeled red banana in her mouth, and climbed a lichened live oak at the far edge of the tall grass, where she sat eating her fruit.

Saul of Tarsus, working the far edge of the rice paddy, spied her from the other side of the shallow pond that ran off from the rice, between the growing grain and the grass, and after a few minutes he waded through the pond—pausing from time to time as though he were simply soaking his feet—yet stealthily moving toward the oak tree where Sara sat. He slowly shinnied up the oak, stopping whenever she peered down at him, till she went on nibbling her banana. Saul of Tarsus felt amorous and he felt hungry, yet not at all sure which desire grabbed him most.

The little girl nervously peered at the chimp ascending and at first did not move because he was not in motion, but when he seemed suddenly to be much too close to her, she dropped the remains of the banana and made shrill little cries, showing her teeth in a frightened grin.

Sara climbed into the crown of the oak, Saul of Tarsus sneakily following her, pretending he wasn't. But now she screeched excitedly until the two adult males across the field leaped off the rock and came charging through the heavy grass to the trees.

Hearing their raucous alarm-barks, Saul of Tarsus hastily slid down the oak tree and knuckle-galloped back to the rice paddy, pursued by the barking baboons. The young chimp waded through the pond to the other side, where he sought the protective company of Melchior, Hattie, and his less adventurous brother.

Melchior testily demanded to know where he had been.

Saul of Tarsus swore he had been attacked by some vicious creatures. The old ape cursed out the two baboons at the edge of the water. "You stupid, dog-face monkeys, go back where you came from."

The male baboons barked raucously at the chimps, then scuttled back to the big rock, where little Sara sat among the adult females, grooming her mother. The mother had swatted her hard when she came back from the oak tree, and the child had yelped, but afterwards calmly chewed a tuber.

Cohn had visited the baboon rock, and though his hopes of communicating with these animals were dim, he had asked where they had come from and how they had survived the Flood. The baboons appeared not to be disturbed by his presence, whether they understood him or not, and went on eating and ignoring him as he questioned them at length. Cohn left, feeling he had accomplished little, and was almost certain that Buz, no matter who had faith, would not be able to teach them anything resembling a spoken language.

It was on this occasion that he named the adult males Max—the one with the bleeding eye, and Arthur—the one with the torn snout; and the look-alike females he named the three Anastasias.

Afterwards Cohn spoke sternly to Luke. "Hattie tells me you were working up a sneak-attack on Sara, the little baboon."

Luke said that Hattie didn't know her mouth from a waterhole. "That wasn't me, that was Saul of Tarsus."

"Was that you stalking the little baboon girl?" Cohn asked Saul of Tarsus, and the chimp breathily replied he thought it was his brother who had stalked her.

"Whoever it was," warned Cohn, "I don't want anybody attempting to terrorize her again."

Saul of Tarsus said all he had wanted to do was play tickle with her.

"Playing with her is one thing, scaring her half to death is something else again. If you want to play, play nice—no harm or threats of harm to an innocent child."

"Not me," said Saul of Tarsus.

"What about you?" Cohn asked Luke.

"Not me either."

Cohn smiled through his grizzled beard. "Why would anyone want to harm a little female baboon?" he asked. "This is a peaceful island. Besides, we're moving into the next civilization."

"Esau told us that baboons don't belong to our tribe," Luke said. "He said that all they are is goddam strangers. That's what he told us both."

"Never mind Esau. Strangers are people God expects us to welcome and live with."

"What for?"

"So we stop being strangers."

"Then why does he make strangers in the first place?"

"To see what we might do about it. What you do right improves you. That's the kind of conditions the Lord has imposed on us. You have to think He means well."

He listened vaguely for a whirlwind from the north and heard only a clear blue sky over a sunlit island of massed trees and multitudes of blooming flowers surrounded by a warm, fragrant sea.

Cohn also spoke to Esau.

"I'm talking to you because you're a chimp of more than ordinary potential, not to speak of unusual physical resources and other useful endowments and attributes. It's not for nothing you're the ranking ape on the island, and since your recent reformation, one of the best workers in the vineyard."

"Which vineyard is that?"

"I use the word metaphorically—the fruitful island as vineyard."

"I am the best," Esau admitted. "Better than Buz or whoever."

Cohn pretended not to have heard "whoever." He told him he was worried about Saul of Tarsus. "He may have been about to do real harm to little Sara, the baboon child who sits with the others on that big rock on the other side of the rice paddy. Somebody said you've been telling him that the baboons don't belong here because they're strangers."

Esau said he had never liked them. "They're monkeys and ought to look like monkeys. Instead, they look like monkeys with dog-heads, I don't go for that."

Cohn then recited the First Admonition, the part about cherishing life.

Esau, after a minute's reflection, said he would try to tolerate the baboons although he didn't naturally take to them. He then asked Cohn if they were expecting a shipment of female chimps in the near future.

Cohn answered it was possible that an unattached female or two—God willing—might one day wander into the neighborhood, but it was impossible to predict when.

Esau said that masturbating gave him a headache and he would prefer something more practical.

"Sublimation is what I advise, considering circumstances," said Cohn. "That's using one's sexual energy creatively—in thought, art, or some satisfying labor."

Esau, after listening with a stunned expression, asked after Mary Madelyn. "How is she doing with her baby?"

"She's doing fine," said Cohn, not liking to talk to him about Mary Madelyn, or the baby.

"You're a lucky prick," said Esau, regarding him enviously. "I bet you get it every night."

Cohn told him to be careful of his language.

Esau rose erect, and with his powerful arms lifted Cohn off the ground in hearty embrace, all but cracking four of his ribs.

Neither of them laughed, though both were laughing.

One day when the sun shone golden, and a summer breeze blew an armada of long white clouds through the cerulean ocean-sky, Sara hopped off the big rock, where the adult baboons had sunned themselves asleep, and Pat and Aloysius were seriously grooming each other, and she danced in the warm grass. She nosed into a patch of bare earth, pushing aside small stones in search of insects but found none.

Sara traveled elegantly through the grass, stopping for a mouthful of dusty water in a small waterhole, then climbed a slender, fragrant, yellow sandalwood and fell asleep in the crook of two upper branches.

Saul of Tarsus, spotting her there, pointed her out to Esau, Buz, Esterhazy, Bromberg, and Luke, who were out prospecting for chimpanzee females, although it was agreed there were none.

Esau at once took charge. He stationed Bromberg, Esterhazy, and Luke at the trunks of three neighboring trees, and ordered Buz to go home.

"Go home yourself," Buz told him.

"This hunt isn't for an intellectual-type chimp. Your brains will get in the way."

"Which hunt are you referring to?"

"You better go home before you fall on your head."

Buz ran off to tell Cohn what was going on, but Cohn wasn't in the cave; he, and Mary Madelyn, carrying Rebekah nursing, were sitting at the beach, watching the waves.

("Suppose a boat came," said Calvin Cohn.

"Could I and Iwanda go with you?" she asked.

"Go where? No boat will ever come.")

Annoyed because nobody was there to hear his news, Buz flung a mango pit into the cave and scampered off when the noise of glass breaking sounded inside.

Esau, his hair thickening as he climbed the sandalwood where Sara lay sleeping on her stomach, as the chimps on the ground tensely watched, with a quick leap forward grabbed the baboon girl. Sara awoke as he touched her, screeching as if she had been set afire, but Esau had her by her hind legs.

He held the screaming, wildly twisting, little baboon, and slammed her head against the tree until the trunk ran blood.

When Max and Arthur, after galloping across the savanna toward Sara's shrill screams, came upon the chimps in the wood, Esau was descending the tree with the body of Sara hanging by its tail from his mouth.

The baboons, with a barking roar, leapt at the apes waiting at the base of the sandalwood, but the chimps, hooting, screaming, fought them off. Luke flung rocks underhand, as Bromberg belabored them with a heavy stick he had picked up. The baboons fled into the bush.

Esau sat on a fallen dead tree, dismembering Sara, the other chimps seated in a silent semicircle, each with his hand formally extended, each getting nothing.

After a solitary meal, relishing every morsel, grunting over the ravishing taste of fresh meat, Esau at length distributed a leg ligament to Saul of Tarsus, a small strip of gut to Esterhazy, the bloody windpipe to Luke, who fruitlessly blew into it; and Bromberg was permitted to suck Sara's eyeballs before Esau began to pry out the brain.

One by one he tossed away the bone fragments of the shattered small skull until he had exposed the pulpy, pinkly-bloodied brain. He plucked it out with his fingers, bit into it, savoring it, chewing slowly, adding a mouthful of leaves Luke had brought him to make the taste of brain last longer. Luke also wanted to keep the delicacy from being too quickly devoured.

At the end of the tastiest meal he remembered since he was a boy in the headlands, Esau handed the remains of little Sara's skeleton to Bromberg—"a nice guy." The other chimpanzees extended their upturned palms, but Bromberg, as he studied the possibilities of the repast, pushed all hands away.

They sat motionless, each concentrating on Bromberg gnawing what was left of flesh on the bones. He handed a few bare bones around, the right arm to Luke, who, Esterhazy complained, had been of no earthly help on the hunt. He got both of Sara's kneecaps. The chimps sniffed the bones, gave them a lick or two, and threw them away.

Esau, lying in the grass, belched resonantly. "I am the Alpha of them all," he murmured as he fell asleep.

His companions sat on the ground studying Sara's naked skeleton.

Cohn, after inspecting the sack containing the remains of Sara that Buz had collected and delivered to him, was horrified, appalled, embittered, saddened.

He thundered against the chimps who had participated in the baboon hunt, calling them depraved killers. For their evil deed he threatened painful punishment. He swore he would flay, uproot, exile them for their brutality, disrespect for the admonitions; for their insensitivity to the welfare of the Island community, to the changed world and altered conditions of earthly survival.

As Cohn railed against them in hoarse, terrifying tones, Buz covered both big ears with his hands, and Mary Madelyn temporarily hid the baby in the bushes.

When he had calmed down and reflected, although grieved, tormented, still angered, Cohn felt he had to deal more subtly with the apes involved in Sara's murder. Rage and curses would get him rage and curses.

These apes, after all, were not the naïve chimpanzees of the past, many of whose recent progenitors had performed as comedians in vaudeville, television, zoos. The island creatures were privileged characters who spoke, and thought, in a complex human tongue, chimps who had improved themselves, and, one had hoped, their lives and lot.

In the schooltree they had heard, and daily discussed, Cohn's lectures on history, science, and literature; and his stories, maxims, recitations, homilies, exhortations—some of which they had spontaneously applauded. And they had had before them the example of their teacher as moral being, family man, author of the Seven Admonitions. When, therefore, would their education take hold, deepen conscience, help them become better, more responsible, living beings? When would they experience that inspired insight that would wake in them what civilization might mean? Who would have thought that this chimpanzee elite would destroy and devour an innocent child?

Cohn planned a new course of lectures, oriented around the matter of significant values. And he made it a point to talk to each chimp.

"Why did you do it, Esterhazy?" Cohn asked the bookkeeperish ape.

"Esau said to."

"Don't you have a will of your own?"

"Not yet," said Esterhazy.

Cohn sat shivah for a week.

*

He would bury Sara's bones.

A funeral was in order, a ceremony of public mourning and respect for life—though they were strangers to her—for the life of the deceased, a child who would never know what it was to be other than a child. A bare few of the chimpanzee community attended, but of those implicated in Sara's murder, only Esterhazy was present.

Mary Madelyn was there, wearing her white dress, which she had to remove every time she nursed the baby. Hattie sat close by them, grooming Mary Madelyn's arms and happily tickling the baby's pink feet so that it giggled or wailed at serious moments, embarrassing its mother and disturbing Cohn.

Melchior, lips puckered, soberly listened to Cohn's graveside eulogy. Buz, thinking his thoughts, was present. And George the gorilla, sitting high in a neighboring tree, looked down at the services, sobered by them. He seemed to have a natural appreciation of funerals. No official Kaddish was recited for the dead child, but Cohn, to George's pleasure, put on a record of his father singing "El Molei Rachameem," a simple prayer for the dead. Dead is dead, who needs more than a song of remembrance?

Reversing his role as digger of bones, Cohn buried the child's skeleton—he had reconstructed it as best he could—near a small natural garden of flowers not far from the schooltree. None of the baboon relatives was at the funeral although Buz had been sent to invite them. He said they hadn't let him approach their rock, confronting him with a yapping chorus of enraged alarm-barks and threats. He hadn't stayed to argue with them.

"They are stupid yokels," said Buz.

*

At the schooltree the next morning, with all scholars present, the killers of Sara sitting together in a tight cluster of males high in the eucalyptus, which gave forth—after a night's fresh rain—an expansive aromatic odor, Cohn, his face raised toward the crown of the tree, spoke directly at Esau, saying certain things. For instance: "If you depreciate lives, the worth of your own diminishes. Therefore remember the Seven Admonitions."

Esau coughed dryly.

Waxing poetic, Cohn said a life gone was a gone life. A flower, or sunrise, no longer existed for it. Neither did a cup of tea—if tea was your dish. The gone life knew it not any longer. No one could describe Nothing, but one's life gone was an aspect, a mode, of nothing. Whoever lived even in Paradise—if that's where she/he had gone—was not here where the weather was more interesting because it varied as the seasons changed.

"Or to put in more practical terms, when you are dead, a fig or sun seed will not tickle your taste buds, and no warm hand will groom you again."

He said that a child—whosesoever—had an inborn, Godgiven right to grow up to be more than a child. "A life—to be a life—must run its course. Thus it achieves freedom of choice, within the usual limitations, but certainly the freedom to imagine the future. Having a future—or thinking you have—waters the gardens of the mind. As though one lives in two places at the same time. Therefore," said Cohn, "it was an evil act of deprivation to destroy little Sara's future."

The apes, though not unmoved, applauded moderately. Mary Madelyn gave a loud "Hurrah," but Buz, detesting homilies—they insulted his intelligence—snorted.

When Cohn, having expressed himself, sat down in his chair, Esau rose, expanding his chest and grabbing a bushy branch to steady himself. More and more he resembled a small gorilla, not necessarily a runt, Cohn thought, but perhaps a runt and a half. When Esau's voice boomed forth, George, assailed by it, dropped out of his cedar and walked away. Esau called him a fat pig, and George blew him some gorilla gas.

Esau proclaimed that every chimp he had known "in the good old days in the highland" had hunted small baboons. It was a perfectly natural, naturally selective, thing to do. The hunt was stimulating and the flesh delicious. "Also it gives me a lift to hear the sound of a crunchy skull that you have batted against something hard.

"And besides that, those baboons are dirty, stinking, thieving monkeys, interfering into everybody's business. They breed like rats and foul up all over the clean bush. If we don't control their population they will squat all over this island and we will have to get off.

"And further to that, all of us are mighty sick and tired of eating so much goddam fruit, plus moldy matzos for dessert."

The male chimps clapped heartily.

"Of course," Esau went on almost congenially, "if there was a piece of sex around instead of that horseass sublimation you are trying to trick on us, we would have something to keep our thoughts going, but the way it has turned out, only our Jewish instructor has sex whenever he might want it, with somebody who happens to be related closer to us; and the rest of us have nothing but our dongs to pull."

Buz stood up and clapped loudly but sat down before Cohn could say anything.

Cohn rose and remarked that since the Day of Devastation, followed by the Late Unlamented Flood, this island had become a privileged place, a sanctuary for the few lives that remained in the world. "And it's got to stay a sanctuary, even if that means a certain amount of food monotony and a few other minor inconveniences."

He asked Esau and his hunter friends to promise they would not terrorize any of the other baboon children; and Esau said if that was what the community wanted, that's what they would get, even if it were against his personal grain.

Cohn did not suggest a voice vote, although tempted to; he wasn't sure he had the votes to win—but he told Esau to raise his right arm and pledge "I will not kill. I will obey the Seven Admonitions."

Esau raised his left arm and solemnly swore he would never again "quote, never again"—kill an innocent female baboon child, and Esterhazy and Bromberg swore along with him.

Pat and Aloysius, groomed immaculate by their mothers, went with them for a root-dig and soon outdistanced and lost the ladies. Climbing a tree to see where they were, they found themselves staring through some branches at Esterhazy, he as astonished as they.

His fur risen, Esterhazy let out a long distress-hoot.

The baboon boys, not waiting to hear the end of it, leaped to the ground and discovered they were being chased by the chimps who had immediately responded to Esterhazy's call—Bromberg, Luke, Saul of Tarsus, and after several minutes, Esau himself. Esterhazy also pursued the baboon boys. Nobody mentioned a pledge of any sort. Besides, that was a pledge not to interfere with a female, and these madly running boys were no girls. Girls couldn't run that fast.

Twisting and darting amid a grove of palms a short distance from the sea, Pat and Aloysius, unable to contend with the speed and agility of the adult chimps racing after them, scuttered up a nut palm, Aloysius behind Pat, both emitting screams as they hastened into the crown.

Esau stationed his men at the base of the bearded date palms nearest the one the boy baboons had gone up, and hand over hand, he climbed the tree after them.

Aloysius, seeing him coming up, flung himself into an adjoining, shorter, broad-crowned palm; and Pat, making a similar large leap, stayed on Aloysius's tail, still scream-barking.

Because Bromberg was stationed at the trunk of this tree, without stopping they jumped into the top of the nearest stout palm—at the bottom of which, they discovered, Esterhazy stood guard.

Esau had plunged after them into the broad-crowned palm.

The baboon children leaped at the trunk of a long palm arced like a scimitar, held tight, and quickly raced up to its feathery small crown. At that moment Max and Arthur, the adult baboons, came roaring into the palm grove with ferocious barking and fangs bared.

They simultaneously attacked Bromberg, who tried fending them off with sharp barks and both arms flailing, but the baboons penetrated his defense and tore at his legs and pink scrotum. Bromberg, shrilly screaming, snarled, and in a moment of pause, hobbled off, then ran, bleeding down his legs.

The adult baboons fought fiercely with Esterhazy, who ran up the long arced palm pursued by Max.

Arthur, noisily jabbing at Luke and Saul of Tarsus protecting each other back to back, snapped at them in feinting leaps, but was afraid to charge two male chimpanzees. They hooted, barked, showed their teeth, and pawed at the jumping baboon, holding him off.

Esau had catapulted himself into the slender curved palm the little boys were in now, both screeching as they peered down at the baboon males on the ground.

Aloysius jumped back onto the shorter

palm, lost his grip on a swishing branch, grabbed and lost another, and tumbled twenty feet to the ground, hitting Luke and knocking him out. Aloysius escaped into the bushes, followed by Arthur. Max soon scampered after them.

Little Pat, still in the palms, hopped into a live oak at the edge of the palm grove, and as Esau swung in after him, jumped again into the grove, still chased by the Alpha Ape. Pat, taking a desperate chance, dove into the bushes below, and as he lay gasping on the ground on his belly, trying to breathe, was pounced on by Saul of Tarsus and Bromberg.

Max and Arthur returned on the run, searching for Pat, but Esau, who had snatched the squirming, terrified boy away from his captors, standing erect, his body hair heavily full, swung the screaming baboon by his legs at the adult baboons. They drew back, snarling, and were at once savaged by Luke and Esterhazy. Max and Arthur rushed into the bushes.

Esau, whirling the boy baboon over his head, slammed him hard against a rock. The breaking skull made the sound of a small explosion. Pat now hung limp in Esau's hand.

Squatting on the ground, facing his hungry companions, he began to peel the bone fragments off the baboon's bloody skull to dig at once for the brain.

Bromberg, still bleeding from wounds on both legs, timidly requested the testicles, and

Esau promised him one if he behaved while he ate his meal.

The twins, their palms extended, in small voices begged for a bit of flesh; and Esau stopped chewing little Pat's remains long enough to give them both a good tickle until they broke into excruciating laughter.

Esau resumed eating the yummy brain after reminding those present what they already knew—that little Pat could in no way be described as a baboon girl.

While strolling with Buz, as Cohn attempted to explain the Second Law of Thermodynamics and his boy corrected his dod's facts, they came upon four chimps silently observing a fifth voraciously feasting on the boy baboon.

Cohn ran furiously into their midst, tore the partially eaten cadaver out of Esau's bloody hands, and with a cry flung it deep into the bushes. Saul of Tarsus watched it in flight, and when it fell, was about to bolt for it, but seeing the other apes sitting frozen, did not move.

"Each devours his neighbor's flesh," Cohn shouted from Isaiah, swearing he had begged them not to repeat this heinous crime.

"Wouldn't you think you owed me some consideration for how comfortable I have helped make your lives? You have work, leisure, free schooling and health care. You have survived a Disastrous Flood and live in comparative peace on an indescribably beautiful island. We have a functioning community and are on the verge of an evolutionary advance, if not breakthrough. And how do you show your appreciation of these advantages? In the murder of children!"

He accused them of ingratitude. He called them hypocrites. "Wasn't it only yesterday that three of you raised your hands in a solemn oath to obey the Seven Admonitions, yet hadn't the slightest intention to do so? You're a disgrace to decent chimpanzees wherever they may be."

They listened with interest as Cohn castigated them. Only Esau was restless as he rubbed the blood off his hairy fingers with oak leaves. One by one he wiped the fingers, then with a broken twig cleaned under his fingernails.

Cohn ran on: "After all the poems and stories we discussed in class regarding the sanctity of life, and after the homily I preached at little Sara's funeral; to wit, a child's right to experience the awakening of sensibility, thought, the discovery of self, and afterwards to emerge in the world in the majesty of youth—despite that, you have with your hands and teeth torn their bodies apart and cannibalized them."

"What the hell are you—some crazy kind of vegetarian?" Esau asked, still cleaning his fingernails.

Cohn called them corrupt and brutish evil-doers, hard-hearted beasts with little understanding or compassion.

"Remember man destroyed himself by his selfishness and indifference to those who were different from, or differed with, him. He scorned himself to death. At least learn that lesson if you want to evade his fate.

"I have no desire to punish you corporally," he announced, "therefore by the authority vested in me as Protector of the Community, I hereby officially exile the three of you—Esau, the falsely redeemed—you fake—and Bromberg, who has no second thought after a limp first—and Esterhazy, coward and fool."

He said he would chastise Luke and Saul of Tarsus at a later date in a manner befitting their age.

They both cheered.

"Quiet," ordered Cohn. "Now, therefore, I order you three to pack your gear and leave this end of the island. If there was another island in the neighboring waters, I would exile you there, provided there was a ferry boat to transport you—but since there isn't another island, so far as I know, I want you to go elsewhere on this, far away and out of sight. If we lay eyes on you again, I warn you of direst consequences."

After he had said this, Cohn felt himself trembling.

The three adult apes glanced uneasily at each other and then Esau rose with a bellow to his full height and advanced on Cohn with four fangs gleaming. Buz, Esterhazy, Bromberg, Luke, and Saul of Tarsus noisily scattered.

Cohn, frozen an instant, began to back up slowly, wishing he had brought along his spear when he had started out for a walk with Buz. What can I do that Esau can't—or doesn't expect? If I try force against his force I won't have much to show, if anything.

He planned at least a quick kick in the groin, and if that worked, to take off for the cave hurriedly, and once there, to shove the defensive wall across the opening. When Esau had left the scene he would sneak out and round up Mary Madelyn and the baby.

Yet Cohn knew that if he got close enough to kick Esau where it hurt, he was close enough to be upended by Esau's longer reach.

The Alpha Ape pounded his chest. "You busybody horseass, you stole my natural food out of my mouth. You possessed my betrothed and forced her to bear your half-breed child. I will break every Jewbone in your head."

He advanced toward Cohn, standing erect, both arms extended, hoot-barking, the ferocity of his expression fearsome.

This is no place for me, thought Cohn, wishing for a slingshot; but he had none, so he retreated, making ugly faces and disgusting noises, but without a frightening mask they had no effect.

"Maybe we ought to talk, Esau. Let's reason together."

He turned to run as the ape pounced on him, snatching Cohn like a fierce lover, lifting him off the ground. Instead of embracing him he flung him down like a dead dog. Cohn grunted in pain and tried to roll into the brush. Esau dragged him forth by his leg and with a snarl fell on him.

"Help—Buz," Cohn cried.

But there was no Buz, until Cohn caught a split-second glimpse of him sitting on an upper branch of a tree, looking down at the combat with absorbed interest, as he peeled an orange.

Life grew dark for Cohn. Death was a white eye centered in a staring black face. That was how he saw Esau, who seemed to be choking him to death. Afterwards he would bash Cohn's skull with a rock and eat his brain as a delicacy. Cohn hoped it poisoned the evil ape.

He himself wandered in Paradise, trying to exit, but all portals were locked. Woe is me, he muttered, how does one get back to life? He had asked this question of the Lord and heard no answer. He heard his own rapid, choked, diminishing breathing.

At this moment of his dying Cohn felt already dead; but Esau, as though he had heard a telephone ring and had decided to answer, loosened his hands on Cohn's neck and fell to the side like a sack of flour. He lay utterly still.

That was no miracle. Mary Madelyn, holding Rebekah in her arm, had sneaked up behind Esau with Cohn's claw hammer, and as the chimps in the trees gazed in stupefaction, had bounced the tool against his head.

That evening, a throat-bruised, hoarse-voiced Cohn bandaged Esau's wound after sewing twenty-one stitches in his scalp; and in the morning the bandaged ape hobbled forth, with a severe headache and small borrowed suitcase, into permanent exile.

Bromberg and Esterhazy had vanished. And Luke and Saul of Tarsus were let off with strong reprimands. Both promised to mend their ways. Buz swore he had been about to drop like Tarzan out of the tree onto Esau's back to rescue Cohn, but Mary Madelyn had got there first.

He did, however, say he hadn't taken kindly to those nasty curses Cohn had laid on the race of chimpanzees.

In a week Cohn paid a census visit to baboon rock and noticed that Aloysius was missing.

"Where's the little baboon boy?" he politely inquired, and the two males roused themselves with malignant roars and showed threatening fangs. The Anastasias, one pregnant, barked mournfully. Cohn hastily ended his visit.

That evening he found little Aloysius's half-eaten, decomposing body smelling up a fig tree full of rotting fruit, the cadaver lying athwart a branch where it had been tossed.

Cohn felt himself a failure.

I have failed to teach these chimpanzees a basic truth. How can they survive if they do to fellow survivors what men did to each other before the Second Flood? How will they evolve into something better than men?

"Who did that terrible thing to Aloysius, Buz?" he asked, and the chimp, devouring a juicy mango, said he had no idea.

"What can we do to dispel the evil rife in this land?"

Buz said it was Cohn's fault for not teaching love. Cohn said he had tried to teach the good life, but it hadn't come to much.

Buz then advised him to remove the false Admonition he had put up on the face of the escarpment.

"Why do you call it false?"

"Because God is love."

Cohn said he wouldn't feel secure promising a loving God. Afterwards he realized he hadn't said that; he had quietly thought it.

He told Buz he was discouraged and would try anything that helped the cause of peace.

When he came out of the woodland the next day, after a count of new fruit trees, to his astonishment but not surprise, Cohn beheld

Buz standing in a balconied enclosure two-thirds of the way up the escarpment, preaching to the chimpanzees assembled below, where the waterfall sometimes sprayed them, but they seemed not to mind.

The chutzpah of that little chimp.

Cohn discovered that Buz, without seeking his consent, had altered the second of the Seven Admonitions on the face of the escarpment. He had removed the "not," and the Admonition read "God is love, God is God."

Cohn decided he would disassemble the second Admonition altogether, except "Remember Him." God, he thought, would not mind so long as he didn't mess around with basics.

It would take a while, given the present spiritual resources of the chimps, to get a new morality in place and working. Even Moses had had trouble, and Isaiah had all but blown his voice crying out against the ethical failures of the Israelites.

At the foot of the escarpment stood the small band of chimpanzees, among them Mary Madelyn holding Rebekah, now very lively. Melchior smoked a homemade cigar rolled from some tough tobacco leaves he had stumbled on on the island. And Hattie remarked she felt she was now Mrs. Melchior, whether they were married or not, even though Melchior had no great interest in sex anymore.

Then Esterhazy and Bromberg slithered in among the others, like escaped convicts who had been slinking around in the rain forest. Yet when they pressed their palms together and sank to their knees, Cohn considered rescinding their sentence to exile. He might give them another chance, but not Esau, because his nature was close to evil.

And Luke, and Saul of Tarsus, were on their knees, praying, but not George the gorilla.

George wasn't there anymore. He had disappeared a few days ago. The rumor was he had trudged off to the headlands, and no one knew for sure if this was a temporary move or one for all time.

Cohn, not without a pang, had watched him lumbering away in the sunset, carrying a small bundle of his belongings at the end of a stick on his shoulder.

"Blessed are the chimpanzees," Buz preached from the terrace of the yellow escarpment, "for they hov inherited the whole earth."

And the chimps below let out a resounding hearty cheer.

Buz later told Cohn he thought that things would go better hereafter in the island community; but Cohn pessimistically reminded him that Christianity, too, hadn't prevented the Holocaust—"the Jewish one I lectured on most recently in class"—nor had it stayed the Day of Devastation.

Buz angrily accused Cohn of never approving anything, pragmatic or spiritual, that he was interested in or had done; and Cohn vehemently denied it.

For an instant they faced each other in anger, right arms upraised, then turned and walked/knuckle-walked away.

After an early supper, as Mary Madelyn was rinsing the wooden platters in the water bucket, Cohn lit the lamp, and pressing his shoulder to the wooden wall, pushed it creaking on its rollers across the mouth of the cave.

"God is   wov," she reminded him. "Why are you shutting the cave off from daywight and fresh air?"

Cohn said he had this feeling that evil persisted in the land, and doubted Buz's sermon would do much to allay it. "It will take a while to get things in order; the atmosphere has been tense since those baboons appeared in the neighborhood. I've been wondering what God is up to."

She asked Cohn when they might get married, and he said they were more or less married. "We must breed daughters."

Cohn held Rebekah in his lap, dressed in a little white sailcloth jumper he had sewed for her; he was about to tell her a bedtime story.

Rebekah, though a half-chimp infant, looked more than half-human. She liked to sit on the ground on her hard little behind, playing with a straw doll Cohn had made for her, whose head she had eaten.

According to Dr. Bünder's book, she was

behind in chimp infant movements, yet ahead in speech. She said dada and mama, and counted to five on one foot and up to ten on the other. She was bright and pretty and chuckled deeply. Her eyes were intensely curious, lively, blue; Cohn was tender to her, enormously fond of his little girl.

He often pondered her fate. Would she live her life out on the island? Was she destined to be the mother of a humanoid-chimpanzoid race if she mated with a full chimp, possibly Buz, someday, if he behaved? Cohn hoped his little girl had been created for a better than ordinary, personally fulfilling, future. At that moment there was a snap-knock on the protective wooden wall, as though someone had thrown a stone against it.

"Open the blosted gate," Buz called from outside. "Whot is there to fear?"

Cohn didn't like the question and would not move the wall.

"Who's out there with you?"

"Just myself."

"What do you want?"

"A condy bar," Buz shouted in frustration, kicking the wall with his bare foot, at once wishing he hadn't.

"Enter," said Cohn.

Mary Madelyn quickly tucked the baby into the crib as Cohn shoved at the wall with his shoulder and slowly pushed it open.

Buz knuckle-limped in. On the way to the

candy box on the shelf he peered at Rebekah in her crib. "I hov forgiven her."

Cohn said he was pleased to hear it, especially since the baby had nothing against him.

"We all feel good will to you, Buz, although we rarely see you except in the schooltree or at public ceremonies."

Buz swallowed a vanilla coconut bar and began chewing a chocolate. He said, with mouth full, it wasn't a kind thing Cohn had done to evict him from his long-standing home.

Cohn reminded him that he had left the cave willingly. "You said you didn't want to live with a squalling brat—you had your private thoughts to think."

Buz seemed to be thinking them. He was, as he ate the candy, staring at Mary Madelyn's bosom in a way that made her blush. She covered the baby with a second blanket.

Cohn got Buz's silver crucifix out of his valise and offered it to him. "You've taken all your worldly goods out of the cave—do you want the cross I've been holding for you?"

"Not now," Buz said. "I hov no pockets on me."

"You can put it around your neck."

"My neck is bigger than it was, the chain wouldn't fit."

Cohn told him to try it.

Buz said no.

Cohn was on the qui vive, when a sulphurous odor assailed his nostrils—nothing like George's, this was a dreadfully foul smell—and his heart sank as he beheld Esau, smirking like the Devil himself, standing in the cave.

Cohn cursed himself for having neglected to roll back the protective wall after Buz had entered. "You knew all the time he hadn't gone into exile," Cohn accused his boy.

Buz said he had heard a rumor but wasn't sure. Cohn was angered and fearful.

With Esau, Esterhazy appeared; and Bromberg, Luke, and Saul of Tarsus entered the cave, wearing clay masks stolen from Cohn's collection, all holding sharp rocks aimed at his head.

Esau, his soiled bandage wrapped around his thick skull, had become heavy-bodied, his face bloated. He looked as if he had spent his time in hiding drinking banana beer. His glazed, reddened eyes were mean-looking.

Mary Madelyn, letting out a cry, snatched the baby from her crib and tried to get out of the cave, but Esterhazy, raising the saber he had found hanging on a hook on the wall, barred her way.

Cohn warned Esterhazy to watch where he pointed the weapon or he would be docked a month's fruit rations.

He then said to Esau, "I have treated you well since you appeared at this end of the island. I pulled a painful tooth and bandaged your wounded head. Be merciful, Esau."

Not mentioning who had wounded the head he had bandaged, Cohn tried to move toward Mary Madelyn and Rebekah and found that his wrists were tightly held by each twin.

Esau, with a sneaky deft movement, snatched Rebekah out of her whimpering mother's arms, and tossed the baby to Bromberg. Rebekah gurgled as she went sailing through the air.

Cohn flung the twins aside and sprang forward to recover the child, as Bromberg threw her to Esterhazy. The bookkeeperish ape caught her in one large hand as Mary Madelyn came rushing at him.

He flipped her to Saul of Tarsus, who passed her to Luke, who scuttled out of the cave.

Mary Madelyn made choking noises of grief as she beat off the twins and burst out of the cave on her fours in pursuit of her daughter.

Cohn prayed for Esau's destruction where he stood—let him drop enormously dead—but nothing came of it. The Alpha Ape lived on in the best of health.

Esau and the other chimps scurried out of the cave, Buz carrying the saber in his teeth. They had left Cohn lying on the ground with a mound of rocks piled on his chest.

"Et tu, Buz?" Cohn was heartbroken beyond his anguish for Rebekah.

He lifted aside one rock after another, not without pressing pain, then rising shakily from the floor, grabbed his iron spear from its rack and charged after the evildoers in the gathering dusk.

The apes met in the gorilla's abandoned cedar near the schooltree and curiously inspected little Rebekah. Esau sat on a high branch, tickling her little pink feet and peeking under the skirt of her jumper to see what was there.

The chimps surrounding him looked on with absorbed interest until Mary Madelyn appeared, distraught, and mumbling to herself. She begged them in heartbroken tones to return her innocent baby and she would give them anything they wanted, promising never again to flee at their approach when she was in heat.

As the sun sank, the island sky turned purple, with zig-zagging rivers of black. The apes wandered like Bedouins from one tree to another with the little girl, as her mother brachiated after them, and Cohn, having abandoned his massive spear, pursued them on foot, his arms extended as he ran, to catch the child if she accidentally fell, or was dropped to the ground by the apes.

He begged them, as he ran, to be merciful. "You may think me a foolishly fond father, but Rebekah—I give you my word—is a gifted child. She's been talking more than a month, and counts to ten on her toes. She's a child of unusual promise, also musically inclined, and may someday be a concert pianist if we can come up with a piano and get a music-education program going.

"It's no exaggeration at all to say that the future of us on this island lives in Rebekah's being, the future of another and—God willing—better civilization, a more idealistic and altruistic one, I certainly hope. She is, as I'm sure you know, half your kind and half mine, and from the unique assortment of her inherited genes, and no doubt of those from one of you in the womb of her maturity—no more than a dozen years from now—the naturally best species of the future will probably be derived. Think of that, gentlemen!

"Please be careful of her—she is our dear child. I urge you to lay her gently on the ground where we can recover her and take her home. I assure you we will reward you all and treat you as heroes."

The apes in the trees seemed to pause in their game to listen to Cohn; and Mary Madelyn, pursuing them without regard for her safety, after a moment of moving stealthily forward, was able to land in the same tree with four of them and almost had her hand on Rebekah, when the astonished Bromberg, come to life, flipped her across the tree aisle to Esau, erect atop a short flowering palm on the left. Esau caught a bad throw but held tight as the other male chimps dived out of the tree into three palms nearby. Mary Madelyn, moaning, sprang into the crown of a nut palm, but Esau had, with a grunt, already leapt forward with the child in his arm, into an adjoining tree.

Cohn, from the ground, promised that if they returned the baby to her loving parents, to either if not both—no doubt this was their ultimate aim, none of them was an intentional kidnapper—he would happily reward them with gifts of 500 sacks of brown rice, about 200 bananas, 48 of which were pulpy red, 56 sweet tangerines, 3 boxes of dried figs, about a ton of sunflower seeds, 32 coconut candy bars, half a large vat of fizzy banana beer, and/or every other object in the cave, including his books, articles of clothing, not excluding his warm poncho; with the cave itself thrown in, and also the outside hut—a joy in summertime—if they mercifully released the little girl, unharmed.

Esau laughed to himself in the deepening dark.

He slung the baby sideways to Esterhazy, who shifted her from one arm to the other and pitched her in an arc over Mary Madelyn's head to Bromberg. Rebekah, for a while wailing faintly, had now ceased crying. In the early evening light she sailed in slow motion through the air, soundlessly in every direction.

It seemed to Cohn that the apes in the trees had become tired or bored; yet their game went on in the dark, and he felt his last hope for his child fall apart.

"Oh, you barbarian beasts! Who but the heartless would tear a little girl from her parents' arms, and not for a minute respond to their piteous pleading—tearful cries, begging—yet relentlessly go on playing a harrowing game of toss-the-baby, without in the least being moved by their distress?

"A curse on your souls, if you have any, and may the Almighty God forever punish you for your wickedness. I pray there's a Third Flood, higher and deeper than the others."

Then Cohn sank to his knees and prayed to God to save his child's life—but after a while rose, thinking, maybe He doesn't like fifty-percent chimps who are fifty-percent human. Or maybe He can't recall the sound of my voice?

Night had descended. The last of light had disappeared in the palm grove, but he could still make out the small white bundle floating through the air from tree to tree, pursued by a fatigued, desolated, brachiating figure approaching closer to the child in motion—until, as darkness grew profound, Rebekah fell, or was pitched at a glowing boulder below; and the two male baboons, Max and Arthur, waiting in the bush, made off with her bloody remains.

It was Cohn's heartbroken impression that no one had willed the event; it had happened because "it was prepared for this," Rashi had said, "from the first six days of creation."

* * *

When the half-moon rose, Cohn found his spear where he had abandoned it. (Would having hurled it at Esau have changed the course of events and saved Rebekah? Would Mary Madelyn, for instance, have caught the baby in her arms if Esterhazy or Bromberg, seeing the spear split Esau's hairy chest, had dropped it in malice or fright?)

Cohn hunted Satan in the nightwood.

He beheld a white bandaged head in the shadowy trees, took aim, and flung the spear with shuddering force. There was a terrible, groaning cry of an ape unwilling to give up life; and a body toppled out of the tree and plummeted to earth.

When Cohn, after spending most of the night searching for Mary Madelyn, came back to bury Esau at daybreak, the ape clutching the spear in his chest, who had bled to death from the massive wound, was not Esau but an albino chimpanzee. Not a god-like mysterious creature—simply a soiled white ape from the headlands, turning black in death; but Cohn felt as though he had murdered a man.

He sought Buz and found him sleeping soundly in a nest in the schooltree. He had forbidden the apes to sleep there, and only Buz had disobeyed. Cohn silently climbed the tree and did what he felt he must.

Buz, awaking with a hoot of fright, found that both his legs had been caught in a noose of vines, and his body trussed to the bough he had built his sleep-nest on. He bared his teeth at Cohn, and Cohn, startled, slapped his face.

"Wot hov I done?" asked the ape. "I om innocent."

Cohn told him he must punish him for betraying his dod, stepmother, and half-sister; he would do it by snapping the wires of his artificial voice-box, depriving him of speech.

Buz, in agitation, begged him not to do *thot*, and Cohn, though grieved, answered he had no choice.

"You betrayed us to those murderous apes. Because of you I unblocked the barrier, and now the child is dead. You were jealous of her and conspired with Esau and the others to kidnap her."

Buz blamed Cohn. "I came for a condy bar for my sweet tooth. You forgot to close the blosted gate."

"You let them lay rocks on my chest. I could barely take a breath, but you did nothing to help me. You left me there in pain. You could have come back but didn't."

Buz swore he had joined their game to spy on them. "I plonned to warn you if they plotted to kill you."

Cohn drew the wire clippers from his pants pocket.

"Please don't take my speech away," Buz

begged. "Take anything but thot. Dr. Bünder wouldn't commit thot nosty crime on his worst enemy. He loved me as a father loves his child."

"I was a father and loved my child. The Lord giveth and taketh away."

Pong pong. Cohn clipped the knotted rusty wires through the hairs on his neck, but not before Buz had groaned, "I om not Buz, my name ist Gottlob."

The apes assembled by habit in the empty schooltree the next morning and threw sun seeds and stones at Cohn's head as he sat on his teaching stool.

He had searched in vain for Mary Madelyn, but she was nowhere to be found. Neither was Esau present, nor had Cohn seen Gottlob again.

As he began to talk the twins booed. Hattie shrilly hooted at him. It sounded like "Hoity-toity."

Cohn was moved to talk about Rebekah, tell stories of what she was like—for a moment attempt to undo in language what had been done to her; to bring her back to life. They listened in silence but when he stopped talking, overcome by grief for his little girl, the twins mocked him. They tore out branches of eucalyptus leaves and, hoo-hooting, showered them on him, together with some sharp small rocks they had carried up the tree in a sack. Hattie and Melchior flung palm nuts at Cohn. He begged them all to fast for the future, and got boos and gurgles in response. It was then he realized the chimpanzees had lost their speech. He hadn't planned it thus. That it had worked out so burdened Cohn's heart.

He hurried to the cave to hide behind his bulwark till things settled down and he figured out what to do next. Was there a way to escape the island? He planned to build a raft on the shore. High tide would float it out.

What if it drifted in the ocean forever? Suppose Cohn and his beard had to live forever on a raft?

As he hastened to the cave, he caught sight of Mary Madelyn in the field beyond the waterfall, this side the rice paddy, her sexual flower risen like a stiff red flag, her white sail dress torn into rags on the grass. She crouched as Esau, eating a bruised banana, mounted her. He pumped once, dismounted carefully, peeled himself another banana.

Then Gottlob, who had been looking on studiously, entered Mary Madelyn twice. Shutting both eyes he concentrated, as he pumped vigorously and dismounted; then he reentered, pumped eight hard deliberate times, and proudly descended. He seemed to have shamed Esau, who had stopped chewing his small banana and would not look him in the eye.

Gottlob pounded his chest and indicated by raising his fist that he was the Alpha Ape.

Esau did not contest the matter.

"Mary Madelyn," Cohn heartbrokenly called to her. "Here I am!"

Sighting him, the three chimpanzees knuckle-ran for the trees.

"Don't forget Romeo and Juliet," he called. "Love, Wov, Lwov!"

He waited for her response but heard nothing. Cohn wondered for a minute if he had gone deaf. Or hadn't she wanted to hear him? She was lost without words.

That night, as he was stuffing his gear into duffel bags, a gang of chimps rammed down his protective wall with a huge log they carried, and poured into the cave, Gottlob leading the way. Cohn had hidden under the bed.

The chimps feasted on fresh and dried fruit, and on cans of food banged open with a hammer or thrown against the wall—tuna, olives, spaghetti, and beans. They tore apart Cohn's threadbare underwear, patched trousers, poncho, and other wearing apparel; destroyed his writing instruments, platters and tumblers, clay masks and flower vases, books and paper. They broke his saber at the hilt, hitting it on the fireplace ledge, and smashed the stock of the 30.06 Winchester by batting it against the rock wall. All the beer they couldn't drink they poured on the ground and sloshed around in. Gottlob put on Cohn's galoshes and waded in the banana beer.

The apes then pulled down, and shattered with the iron spear, the wooden storage shelves Cohn had built on first arriving on the island.

Esau, with the claw hammer that had bloodied his head, smashed all the cantor's old records, and in three savage strokes demolished the portable phonograph. Its insides hung out.

The apes apprehended Cohn, binding his arms with a metal chain he had once tied a trunk with, and they looped a rope around his neck. As they tightly tied him up—his arms behind his back, his legs, on Gottlob's insistence, trussed together—they laughed, screamed, barked, hooted, filling the echoing cave with impossible noise. But in the place where the wrecked phonograph stood, a rabbinic voice recited the law.

God's Mercy

)))|(((

In the day they ascended in sunlight, and at night through a cloud of stars drenching the mountainside.

Cohn's wrists were bound by leather thongs; he carried a bundle of split wood against his chest. A noose hung loose around his skinny neck, its frayed rope trailing behind him as he plodded up the stone mountain. He wore his white kitl, not a warm garment this cold night.

Buz trailed behind him, walking erect, a terry-cloth turban on his head and a pair of Cohn's old sandals on his feet.

At a turn in the narrow road they met a beggar, a surprise to all.

He stretched forth his bony seven-fingered

hand, but Cohn said he couldn't possibly reach into his pocket because his hands were bound.

"So say it in words."

"My words are questions."

"Ask."

"For instance, are you the Lord's Messenger? Or possibly the Messiah?"

"I am a beggar who begs."

"Begs what?"

"A blessing."

"I wish I had one to give."

"Oho," said the beggar, disappearing in a cloud of mist as deep as an avalanche of snow.

Cohn had heard of such encounters on mountain roads.

"Who was that?" he asked anyway. "Pong," was all Buz said.

Cohn wondered what would happen if he tried running down the mountain, but Buz ran faster than he and if by chance he stepped on Cohn's trailing rope it could break his neck.

So he climbed the stone mountain in his bare feet, holding the split wood against his chest.

"Buz," said Cohn, "you are my beloved son, tell me where we are going. I think I know but would like you to say so."

"Pong."

At an altitude where five evergreens grew in a bunch they came upon an open cave with an altar gleaming within.

Cohn dropped the wood on the ground and relieved himself against the mountain before gathering up the pieces and approaching the altar.

Buz seemed to look at a watch he didn't have and pointed it was time.

"Where's this ram in the thicket?" asked Cohn with a bleat.

Buz wagged his finger at his dod.

Though he had known, Cohn turned icy cold. "Am I to be the burnt offering?"

"Pong."

Buz laid the wood in an orderly row on the altar and applied a match to the dried logs. He poured spices and myrrh into the smoke. The flames sprang up, crackling in a foreign tongue.

"Untie my hands and I won't move, I promise you. I shan't blemish the sacrifice. If that's what I am, that's what I am."

Buz indicated Cohn kneel. He bent his knees to show how.

"I wouldn't do this if you weren't my beloved son."

Cohn knelt before the fire, waiting for a naysaying angel who never appeared. Unless one had come and gone? You can't depend on angels.

Buz pulled his father's head back by his long hair, exposing his neck, aiming at his throat with a stone knife.

Blood, to their astonishment, spurted forth an instant before the knife touched Cohn's flesh.

"Poong," said Buz, but it came to nothing.

Who could tell whether it meant yes, no, or maybe.

Cohn lay still on the floor of the cave waiting to be lifted onto the flames. By the golden dark-light of the fire he could see that his long white beard was flecked with spots of blood.

"Merciful God," he said, "I am an old man. The Lord has let me live my life out."

He wept at the thought. Maybe tomorrow the world to come?

In a tall tree in the valley below, George the gorilla, wearing a mud-stained white yarmulke he had one day found in the woods, chanted, "Sh'ma, Yisroel, the Lord our God is one."

In his throaty, gruff voice he began a long Kaddish for Calvin Cohn.